Why the Fish
Laughed
&
Other Stories

Publications from
The Scheherazade Foundation

The Secrets of Scheherazade
An Ordered Experience
Tale of a Lantern & Other Stories
The Elephant & The Tortoise & Other Stories
The Monkey's Fiddle & Other Stories
Ghost of the Violet Well & Other Stories
Many Wise Fools & Other Stories
The Frog Prince & Other Stories
The Three Lemons & Other Stories
The Twelve-Headed Griffin & Other Stories
The Antelope Boy & Other Stories
Why the Fish Laughed & Other Stories
Two Cats & Other Stories
Three Stories
The Twilight of the Gods & Other Stories
The Son of Seven Queens & Other Stories
The Moon Maiden & Other Stories
The Metamorphosis & Other Stories
The Celestial Sisters & Other Stories
Tales from the Arabian Nights I
East of the Sun, West of the Moon & Other Stories
The Well at the End of the World & Other Stories

WHY THE FISH LAUGHED
&
OTHER STORIES

Edited & Introduced by

TAHIR SHAH

The Scheherazade Foundation

The Scheherazade Foundation CIC
85 Great Portland Street
London
W1W 7LT
United Kingdom
www.SF.Charity
info@SF.Charity

First published by The Scheherazade Foundation CIC, 2023

WHY THE FISH LAUGHED
&
OTHER STORIES

Why the Fish Laughed
Indian Fairy Tales
Joseph Jacobs
G. P. Putnam's Sons
1910

The Origin of the Winds
A Treasury of Eskimo Tales
Clara Kern Bayliss
Thomas Y. Crowell Co.
1922

Mooregoo the Mopoke, & Bahloo the
Moon
*Folklore of the Noongahburrahs as Told
to the Piccaninnies*
K. Langloh Parker
David Nutt & Co.
1896

Fishsave
Child-life in Japan
M. Chaplin Ayrton
William Elliot Griffis
D.C. Heath & Co
1901

The Sparrow & the Bush
Cossack Folk Tales
R. Nisbet Bain
George G. Harrap & Co.
1894

The Princess on the Glass Hill
East of the Sun & West of the Moon
Peter Christen Asbjørnsen & Jørgen
Engebretsen Moe
1910
George H. Doran Co.

The Sea Moans
Fairy Tales from Brazil
Elsie Spicer Eells
Dodd, Mead & Company, Inc.
1917

The Perfidious Vizier
Oriental Folklore & Legends
Charles John Tibbitts
W. W. Gibbings Ltd.
1889

The Bird-lover
The Indian Fairy Book
Cornelius Mathews
Allen Brothers Inc.
1869

The Tortoise with a Pretty Daughter
Folk-Stories from Southern Nigeria
Elphinstone Dayrell
Longmans, Green & Co.
1910

The Jelly Fish Takes a Journey
Green Willow & Other Japanese Fairy Tales
Grace James
Macmillan & Co.
1912

Jack the Giant-killer
English Fairy Tales
Joseph Jacobs
G. P. Putnam's Sons
1892

The Enchanted Mule
Tales From the Lands of Nuts & Grapes
Charles Sellers
Simpkin, Marshall & Co.
1888

The Fisherman's Son & the Gruagach of Tricks
Myths & Folk-Lore of Ireland
Jeremiah Curtin
Sampson Low & Co.
1890

Blondine Lost
Old French Fairy Tales
Comtesse de Ségur
The Penn Publishing Co.
1920

The various authors listed above assert the right to be identified as the Authors of the Work in accordance with the Copyright, Designs and Patents Act 1988.
A CIP catalogue record for this title is available from the British Library.

ISBN 978-1-915311-23-8

CONTENTS

Series Introduction

FROM EARLIEST CHILDHOOD, I was told stories.

Of course, I was – most children are told stories.

After all, telling children stories is one of the foundations that makes their early experiences a childhood.

But as I think back to the first years of my own life, I find myself reeling from the sheer quantity of stories my infant ears took in.

Whereas other children my age were told stories for amusement, my parents (and the people they associated with) recounted the endless streams of tales for a different reason.

In their opinion, stories – and the ability to tell them – were part of an ancient alchemy... a way of processing complex ideas, of solving problems, and of developing the human mind.

My father, the writer and thinker Idries Shah, believed that folklore was the single most important breakthrough ever developed by the human species. The way he saw it, the rise of stories was as consequential as the development of the languages in which they were told.

He would say that, without stories and storytelling, humanity would never have evolved in the way that it has – and that the folktales, which form a bedrock of ancient societies, are more precious than any physical artefact unearthed on an archaeological dig.

As the years of my own childhood slipped by, I found myself unbothered to work out the hidden layers within treasuries of stories – what my father called 'instruction manuals to the world'. Like everyone else, I simply absorbed the individual tales, delighting in them.

And that's it – the key point, the genius of stories and storytelling.

It's a thing I only grasped in adulthood… something that fascinates me deeply.

In the same way you can jump into a car and drive across the country without giving a second thought to the engine or how it works, you can appreciate stories without understanding the hidden layers and devices that make them what they are.

Stories are all around us.

They're in the TV and movies we so adore, in the video games we play, and of course in the books we read. They're in newspapers and magazines, too; in the conversations we share with old friends, and with new ones. They're on our mobile phones, in aeroplanes, in submarines, and even in our dreams.

Our obsession with, and craving for, stories rests squarely with the way we are so absorbed by them, just as it does with the way we don't need to continually consider how and why they work.

Throughout my life, I've devoted an increasing amount of time to gathering stories from all corners of the world.

It began in my late teens, when I began to criss-cross the continents in a crazed preoccupation with folklore. I developed a first-hand love affair with societies that, over millennia, gave birth to their own astonishing traditions of stories and storytelling.

Most of the time, when reading or listening to stories, we forget that these tales have been shaped through the passage of time. Like pebbles in a river smoothed by rushing waters, they were honed through centuries of telling and retelling.

When I was twelve years old, my father published a masterwork, *World Tales*. The first edition was very large and featured hundreds of original illustrations. The book was unlike any that had come before, for it detailed the provenance and history of each story told.

At bedtime one night, he presented me with an advanced copy. For as long as I could remember, my father had been talking about the project.

Having an actual copy in my hands at last was thrilling beyond words.

Peering down at me sternly, my father said:

'This is far more than a book, Tahir Jan. It's the foundation stone of a great building... a building that *is* human culture. As you grow older, and as you go out into the world, you will understand that the folklores contained between the covers of *World Tales* have brought amusement and educated, and have solved problems when they were needed most of all.'

My father was right.

When I eventually headed out into the wilds of the world for the first time, I discovered the stories contained in *World Tales* for myself, along with a great many more. Just as he said, the stories published in his treasury were the warp and weft threads of society. Stories are the matrix on which culture itself is based – a framework that enables daily life to continue as smoothly as it does.

In this series of books, we have drawn together stories from all over the world. It's a mission begun decades ago by *World Tales*.

Some of the pieces will be known to you, and others will not.

Some will be easy to comprehend, while others will be challenging, or even nonsensical.

I'd now like to note something else...

The Occidental world seems to assume stories must appear in certain regimented ways – presented with a well-defined beginning, a middle, and an end. You know what I mean: the protagonist winning against all odds, and the happy ending to it all.

In the ancient tradition of teaching stories, the kind recounted for an eternity around campfires in the desert and in longhouses deep in the jungle, there's no such standardisation.

Rather, there's usually a hotchpotch of conflicting threads: stories without a straight linear narrative but with an underlying turbulence that gets the reader, or the listener, to sit up and think.

At The Scheherazade Foundation, we are preoccupied with the way we can extract knowledge from stories – either deliberately, or in a less structured way.

We hold the firm opinion that, in order to remove the marrow from the bone stories are best served up in the way as they were passed from one generation to the next throughout human history.

In this series, we have drawn together tales that were gathered in particular during the nineteenth and early twentieth centuries. Spanning a vast range of cultures, they offer an extraordinary glimpse into the societies from which they are drawn – societies that were often changed shortly afterwards by social upheaval, technologies, and war.

Indeed, the fact any of them were recorded at all is a thing of wonder.

Intriguingly, some of the tales will now appear dated because vocabulary and writing styles have altered. But the fact that they seem old-fashioned is of great interest – proof of the way stories are constantly changing and evolving from one era to the next.

Over the last thirty years, I've gathered hundreds of tales on my own journeys, most of them spoken directly into my ears by storytellers and fellow travellers, by wizened old men in the middle of nowhere, and by anyone else good enough to indulge my pleas.

On all those zigzagging adventures, one story sticks out, tantalising me whenever I turn it around my head.

It was called 'The Man Who Turned into a Cat'.

The reason I mention it here is not because it was an especially fine tale, but rather because, from that moment, it affected the way I perceive the world.

It was as though I were a lock and that, by hearing the tale, a key had been slipped into me and turned.

Since first receiving it, I've never been quite the same, my state of consciousness having been flipped inside out.

The fellow traveller who recounted 'The Man Who Turned into a Cat' was lost in shadow, no more than a fragment of his left cheek protruding shyly into the light.

We were sitting on low divans in a teahouse in the ancient Afghan city of Herat.

When the tale had been whispered, I sat there in silence for a long while.

'What have you done to me?' I asked after a long pause.

The fellow traveller offered half a smile.

'*I* didn't do anything,' he replied. 'It's the story that's affected you – a story that I myself first heard when I was a child playing in the orchards of Balkh.'

Peering into the shadow, my eyes widened.

'I don't understand,' I said feebly. 'After all, it's not an especially grand story. There wasn't even a jinn.'

The traveller's mouth eased out from the shadows.

Very slowly, it grinned.

'Tales containing the greatest sustenance for a soul speak in the softest voice,' he said.

Tahir Shah

Why the Fish Laughed

AS A CERTAIN fisherwoman passed by a palace crying her fish, the queen appeared at one of the windows and beckoned her to come near and show what she had. At that moment, a very big fish jumped about in the bottom of the basket.

'Is it a he or a she?' inquired the queen. 'I wish to purchase a she fish.'

On hearing this the fish laughed aloud.

'It's a he,' replied the fisherwoman, and proceeded on her rounds.

The queen returned to her room in a great rage; and on coming to see her in the evening, the king noticed that something had disturbed her.

'Are you indisposed?' he said.

'No; but I am very much annoyed at the strange behaviour of a fish. A woman brought me one today, and on my inquiring whether it was a male or female, the fish laughed most rudely.'

'A fish laughed! Impossible! You must be dreaming.'

'I am not a fool. I speak of what I have seen with my own eyes and have heard with my own ears.'

'Passing strange! Be it so. I will inquire concerning it.'

On the morrow, the king repeated to his vizier what his wife had told him, and bade him investigate the matter, and be ready with a satisfactory answer within six months, on pain of death. The vizier promised to do his best, though he felt almost certain of failure. For five months, he laboured indefatigably to find a reason for the laughter of the fish. He sought everywhere and from everyone. The wise and learned, and they who were skilled in magic and in all manner of trickery, were consulted. Nobody, however, could explain the matter; and so, he returned broken-hearted to his house, and began to arrange his affairs in prospect of certain death, for he had had sufficient experience of the king to know that His Majesty would not go back from his threat. Amongst other things, he advised his son to travel for a time, until the king's anger should have somewhat cooled.

The young fellow, who was both clever and handsome, started off whithersoever kismet might lead him. He had been gone some days, when he fell in with an old farmer, who also was on a journey to a certain village. Finding the old man very pleasant, he asked him if he might accompany him, professing to be on a visit to the same place. The old farmer agreed, and they walked along together. The day was hot, and the way was long and weary.

'Don't you think it would be pleasanter if you and I sometimes gave one another a lift?' said the youth.

'What a fool the man is!' thought the old farmer.

Presently they passed through a field of corn ready for the sickle, looking like a sea of gold as it waved to and fro in the breeze.

8

'Is this eaten or not?' said the young man.

Not understanding his meaning, the old man replied, 'I don't know.'

After a little while the two travellers arrived at a big village, where the young man gave his companion a clasp-knife, and said, 'Take this, friend, and get two horses with it; but mind and bring it back, for it is very precious.'

The old man, looking half amused and half angry, pushed back the knife, muttering something to the effect that his friend was either a fool himself or else trying to play the fool with him. The young man pretended not to notice his reply, and remained almost silent till they reached the city, a short distance outside which was the old farmer's house. They walked about the bazar and went to the mosque, but nobody saluted them or invited them to come in and rest.

'What a large cemetery!' exclaimed the young man.

'What does the man mean,' thought the old farmer, 'calling this largely populated city a cemetery?'

On leaving the city, their way led through a cemetery where a few people were praying beside a grave and distributing chapatis and kulchas to passersby, in the name of their beloved dead. They beckoned to the two travellers and gave them as much as they would.

'What a splendid city this is!' said the young man.

'Now, the man must surely be demented!' thought the old farmer. 'I wonder what he will do next? He will be calling the land water, and the water land; and be speaking of light where there is darkness, and of darkness when it is light.'

However, he kept his thoughts to himself.

Presently, they had to wade through a stream that ran along the edge of the cemetery. The water was rather deep, so the old farmer took off his shoes and pyjamas and crossed over; but the young man waded through it with his shoes and pyjamas on.

'Well! I never did see such a perfect fool, both in word and in deed,' said the old man to himself.

However, he liked the fellow; and thinking that he would amuse his wife and daughter, he invited him to come and stay at his house as long as he had occasion to remain in the village.

'Thank you very much,' the young man replied, 'but let me first enquire, if you please, whether the beam of your house is strong.'

The old farmer left him in despair and entered his house laughing.

'There is a man in yonder field,' he said, after returning their greetings. 'He has come the greater part of the way with me, and I wanted him to put up here as long as he had to stay in this village. But the fellow is such a fool that I cannot make anything out of him. He wants to know if the beam of this house is all right. The man must be mad!' and saying this, he burst into a fit of laughter.

'Father,' said the farmer's daughter, who was a very sharp and wise girl, 'this man, whosoever he is, is no fool, as you deem him. He only wishes to know if you can afford to entertain him.'

'Oh! Of course,' replied the farmer. 'I see. Well perhaps you can help me to solve some of his other mysteries. While we were walking together, he asked whether he should carry me or I should carry him, as he thought that would be a pleasanter mode of proceeding.'

'Most assuredly,' said the girl. 'He meant that one of you should tell a story to beguile the time.'

'Oh yes. Well, we were passing through a cornfield, when he asked me whether it was eaten or not.'

'And didn't you know the meaning of this, father? He simply wished to know if the man was in debt or not; because, if the owner of the field was in debt, then the produce of the field was as good as eaten to him; that is, it would have to go to his creditors.'

'Yes, yes, yes; of course! Then, on entering a certain village, he bade me take his clasp knife and get two horses with it and bring back the knife again to him.'

'Are not two stout sticks as good as two horses for helping one along on the road? He only asked you to cut a couple of sticks and be careful not to lose his knife.'

'I see,' said the farmer. 'While we were walking over the city, we did not see anybody that we knew, and not a soul gave us a scrap of anything to eat, till we were passing the cemetery; but there some people called to us and put into our hands some chapatis and kulchas; so my companion called the city a cemetery, and the cemetery a city.'

'This also is to be understood, father, if one thinks of the city as the place where everything is to be obtained, and of inhospitable people as worse than the dead. The city, though crowded with people, was as if dead, as far as you were concerned; while, in the cemetery, which is crowded with the dead, you were saluted by kind friends and provided with bread.'

'True, true!' said the astonished farmer. 'Then, just now, when we were crossing the stream, he waded through it without taking off his shoes and pyjamas.'

'I admire his wisdom,' replied the girl. 'I have often thought how stupid people were to venture into that swiftly flowing stream and over those sharp stones with bare feet. The slightest stumble and they would fall and be wetted from head to foot. This friend of yours is a most wise man. I should like to see him and speak to him.'

'Very well,' said the farmer; 'I will go and find him, and bring him in.'

'Tell him, father, that our beams are strong enough, and then he will come in. I'll send on ahead a present to the man, to show him that we can afford to have him for our guest.'

Accordingly, she called a servant and sent him to the young man with a present of a basin of ghee, twelve chapatis, and a jar of milk, and the following message: 'O friend, the moon is full; twelve months make a year, and the sea is overflowing with water.'

Halfway, the bearer of this present and message met his little son, who, seeing what was in the basket, begged his father to give him some of the food. His father foolishly complied. Presently he saw the young man and gave him the rest of the present and the message.

'Give your mistress my salam,' he replied, 'and tell her that the moon is new, and that I can only find eleven months in the year, and the sea is by no means full.'

Not understanding the meaning of these words, the servant repeated them word for word, as he had heard them, to his mistress; and thus, his theft was discovered, and he was severely punished. After a little while, the young man appeared with the old farmer. Great attention was shown to him, and he was treated in every way as if he were the son of a great man, although his humble host knew nothing of his origin. At length, he told them everything – about the laughing of the fish, his father's threatened execution, and his own banishment – and asked their advice as to what he should do.

'The laughing of the fish,' said the girl, 'which seems to have been the cause of all this trouble, indicates that there is a man in the palace who is plotting against the king's life.'

'Joy, joy!' exclaimed the vizier's son. 'There is yet time for me to return and save my father from an ignominious and unjust death, and the king from danger.'

The following day he hastened back to his own country, taking with him the farmer's daughter. Immediately on arrival he ran to the palace and informed his father of what he had heard. The poor vizier, now almost dead from the expectation of death, was at once carried to the king, to whom he repeated the news that his son had just brought.

'Never!' said the king.

'But it must be so, Your Majesty,' replied the vizier; 'and in order to prove the truth of what I have heard, I pray you to call together all the maids in your palace, and order them to jump over a pit, which must be dug. We'll soon find out whether there is any man there.'

The king had the pit dug and commanded all the maids belonging to the palace to try to jump it. All of them tried, but only one succeeded. That one was found to be a man!!

Thus was the queen satisfied, and the faithful old vizier saved.

Afterwards, as soon as could be, the vizier's son married the old farmer's daughter; and a most happy marriage it was.

From: Indian Fairy Tales

The Origin of the Winds

In a village on the lower Yukon lived a man and his wife who had no children. One day the woman said to her husband, 'Far out on the tundra there grows a solitary tree. Go to that and bring back a piece of the trunk and make a doll from it. Then it will seem that we have a child.'

The man went out of the house and saw a long track of bright light like that made by the moon shining on snow, leading off across the tundra in the direction he had been told to take. It was the Milky Way. Along this path he travelled far away, until he saw before him a beautiful object shining in the bright light. Going up to it, he found it was the tree of which he came in search. The tree was small, so he took his hunting knife, cut off a part of the trunk, and carried the fragment home.

He sat down in the house and carved out from the wood an image of a small boy, and his wife made two suits of clothing for it and dressed it in one of them, 'saving the other to put on when he had soiled the first,' she said.

'Now, Father, make your little boy a set of toy dishes,' she said.

'I see no use in all this trouble. We will be no better off than we were in the first place,' said the man.

15

'Why, yes, we are already better off,' said the wife.

'Before we had the doll, we had nothing to talk about except ourselves. Now we have the doll to talk about and to amuse us.'

To please her, the husband made the toy dishes, and she placed the doll in the seat of honour on the bench opposite the door, with the dishes full of food and water before it.

When the couple had gone to bed that night the room was very dark, and they heard several low, whistling sounds.

'Do you hear that? It is the doll,' said the woman, shaking her husband till he awakened.

They got up at once and, making a light, saw that the Doll had eaten the food and drunk the water, and that its eyes were moving. The woman caught it up with delight and fondled and played with it for a long time. When she became tired, she put it back on the bench and they went to bed again.

In the morning when they got up the Doll was gone. They looked for it all around the house but could not find it. Then they went outside, and there were its tracks leading away from the door. They followed the tracks to the creek and along the bank to a place outside the village, where they ended; for from this place the Doll had gone up the Milky Way on the path of light upon which the man had gone to find the tree.

Doll travelled along the bright path till he came to the edge of day, where the sky comes down to the earth and walls in the light. Close beside him, in the east, he saw a skin cover fastened over a hole in the sky wall. The skin was bulging inward as if some strong force on the other side were pushing it.

'It is very quiet here. I think a little wind would make it livelier,' said the Doll, drawing his knife and cutting the cover loose on one side of the hole. At once a strong wind blew through, every now and then bringing with it a live reindeer. Looking through the hole, Doll saw beyond the wall another world like the earth. He drew the cover over the hole again.

'Do not blow too hard,' he said to the wind. 'Sometimes blow hard, sometimes light, and sometimes do not blow at all.'

Then he got upon the sky wall and walked along till he came to the southeast. Here another opening was covered like the first, and the covering was bulging inward. When he cut this covering loose a gale swept in bringing reindeer, trees, and bushes. He quickly covered the hole and said to the gale, 'You are too strong. Sometimes blow hard, sometimes light, and sometimes do not blow at all. The people on earth will want variety.'

Again walking along the sky wall, he came to a hole in the south, and when this covering was cut, a hot wind came rushing in carrying rain and spray from the great sea lying beyond the sky-hole on that side. Doll closed this opening and talked to the wind as before.

Then he passed on to the west where there was another hole which admitted heavy rainstorms, with sleet and spray from the ocean. When he had closed this and given the wind its instructions he went on to the northwest. There, when he cut away the covering, a cold blast came rushing in, bringing snow and ice, so that he was chilled to the bone and half frozen, and he made haste to close the hole as he had the others.

He started to go along the sky wall to the north, but the cold became more and more severe until at last, he was obliged to leave the wall and make a circuit to the southward, going back to the north only when he came opposite the opening. There the cold was so intense that he waited some time before he could muster courage to cut the cover away. When he did so, a fearful blast rushed in, carrying great masses of snow and ice, strewing it over the entire plain of the earth. It was so bitter that he closed the hole very quickly and told the wind from that direction to come only in the middle of the winter so that the people might not be taken unawares, and might be prepared for it.

From there, he hastened down to warmer climes in the middle of the earth plain, where, looking up, he saw that the sky was supported by long, slender, arching poles, like those of a conical lodge, but made of some beautiful material unknown to him. Journeying on, he finally came to the village from which he started and went into his own home.

Doll lived in this village for a very long time; for when the foster parents who had made him died, he was taken by other people of the village and so lived on for many generations, until he finally died. Since his death, parents have made dolls for their children in imitation of the Doll who first opened the wind-holes of the sky and regulated all the six winds of earth.

From: A Treasury of Eskimo Tales

Mooregoo the Mopoke, &
Bahloo the Moon

MOOREGOO THE MOPOKE had been camped away by himself for a long time.

While alone, he had made a great number of boomerangs, nullah-nullahs, spears, neilahmans, and opossum rugs. Well had he carved the weapons with the teeth of opossums, and brightly had he painted the inside of the rugs with coloured designs, and strongly had he sewn them with the sinews of opossums, threaded in the needle made of the little bone taken from the leg of an emu. As Mooregoo looked at his work he was proud of all he had done.

One night Babloo the moon came to his camp, and said: 'Lend me one of your opossum rugs.'

'No. I lend not my rugs.'

'Then give me one.'

'No. I give not my rugs.'

Looking round, Bahloo saw the beautifully carved weapons, so he said, 'Then give me, Mooregoo, some of your weapons.'

'No, I give, never, what I have made, to another.'

Again Bahloo said, 'The night is cold. Lend me a rug.'

'I have spoken,' said Mooregoo. 'I never lend my rugs.'

Barloo said no more, but went away, cut some bark and made a dardurr for himself. When it was finished and he safely housed in it, down came the rain in torrents. And it rained without ceasing until the whole country was flooded. Mooregoo was drowned. His weapons floated about and drifted apart, and his rugs rotted in the water.

From: Folklore of the Noongahburrahs as Told to the Piccaninnies

Fishsave

THERE WAS ONCE upon a time a little baby whose father was Japanese ambassador to the court of China, and whose mother was a Chinese lady.

While this child was still in its infancy, the ambassador had to return to Japan. So, he said to his wife: 'I swear to remember you and to send you letters by the ambassador that shall succeed me; and as for our baby, I will despatch someone to fetch it as soon as it is weaned.'

Thus saying, he departed.

Well, embassy after embassy came (and there was generally at least a year between each), but never a letter from the Japanese husband to the Chinese wife. At last, tired of waiting and of grieving, she took her boy by the hand, and sorrowfully leading him to the seashore, fastened round his neck a label bearing the words, 'The Japanese ambassador's child.'

Then she flung him into the sea in the direction of the Japanese Archipelago, confident that the paternal tie was one which it was not possible to break, and that therefore father and child were sure to meet again.

One day, when the former ambassador, the father, was riding by the beach of Naniwa (where afterward was built the city of Osaka), he saw something white floating out at sea, looking like a small island. It floated nearer, and he looked more attentively. There was no doubt about its being a child. Quite astonished, he stopped his horse and gazed again. The floating object drew nearer and nearer still.

At last with perfect distinctness, it was perceived to be a fair, pretty little boy, of about four years old, impelled onward by the waves.

Still closer inspection showed that the boy rode bravely on the back of an enormous fish. When the strange rider had dismounted on the strand, the ambassador ordered his attendants to take the manly little fellow in their arms, when lo, and behold! there was the label round his neck, on which was written, 'The Japanese ambassador's child.'

'Oh, yes,' he exclaimed, 'it must be my child and no other, whom its mother, angry at having received no letters from me, must have thrown into the sea. Now, owing to the indissoluble bond tying together parents and children, he has reached me safely, riding upon a fish's back.'

The air of the little creature went to his heart, and he took and tended him most lovingly.

To the care of the next embassy that went to the court of China, he entrusted a letter for his wife, in which he informed her of all the particulars; and she, who had quite believed the child to be dead, rejoiced at its marvellous escape.

The child grew up to be a man, whose handwriting was beautiful.

Having been saved by a fish, he was given the name of 'Fishsave'.

From: Child-life in Japan

The Sparrow & the Bush

A SPARROW ONCE flew down upon a bush and said, 'Little bush, give good little sparrow a swing.'

'I won't!' said the little bush.

Then the sparrow was angry, and went to the goat and said, 'Goat, goat, nibble bush, bush won't give good little sparrow a swing.'

'I won't!' said the goat.

Then the sparrow went to the wolf and said, 'Wolf, wolf, eat goat, goat won't nibble bush, bush won't give good little sparrow a swing.'

'I won't!' said the wolf.

Then the sparrow went to the people and said, 'Good people, kill wolf, wolf won't eat goat, goat won't nibble bush, bush won't give good little sparrow a swing.'

'We won't!' said the people.

Then the sparrow went to the Tartars and said, 'Tartars, Tartars, slay people, people won't kill wolf, wolf won't eat goat, goat won't nibble bush, bush won't give good little sparrow a swing.'

But the Tartars said,

'We won't slay the people!' and the people said,

'We won't kill the wolf!' and the wolf said,

'I won't eat the goat!' and the goat said,

'I won't nibble the bush!' and the bush said,

'I won't give the good little sparrow a swing.'

'Go!' said the bush, 'to the fire, for the Tartars won't slay the people, and the people won't kill the wolf, and the wolf won't eat the goat, and the goat won't nibble the bush, and the bush won't give the dear little sparrow a swing.'

But the fire also said, 'I won't!' (they were all alike) – 'go to the water,' said he.

Go the sparrow went to the water and said, 'Come water, quench fire, fire won't burn Tartars, Tartars won't slay people, people won't kill wolf, wolf won't eat goat, goat won't nibble bush, bush won't give good little sparrow a swing.'

But the water also said, 'I won't!'

So, the sparrow went to the ox and said, 'Ox, ox, drink water, water won't quench fire, fire won't burn Tartars, Tartars won't slay people, people won't kill wolf, wolf won't eat goat, goat won't nibble bush, bush won't give little sparrow a swing.'

'I won't!' said the ox.

Then the sparrow went to the poleaxe and said, 'Poleaxe, poleaxe, strike ox, ox won't drink water, water won't quench fire, fire won't burn Tartars, Tartars won't slay people, people won't kill wolf, wolf won't eat goat, goat won't nibble bush, bush won't give little sparrow a swing.'

'I won't!' said the poleaxe.

So, the sparrow went to the worms and said, 'Worms, worms, gnaw poleaxe, poleaxe won't strike ox, ox won't drink water, water won't quench fire, fire won't burn Tartars, Tartars won't slay people, people won't kill wolf, wolf won't eat goat, goat won't nibble bush, bush won't give little sparrow a swing.'

'We won't!' said the worms.

Then the sparrow went to the hen and said, 'Hen, hen, peck worms, worms won't gnaw poleaxe, poleaxe won't strike ox, ox won't drink water, water won't quench fire, fire won't burn Tartars, Tartars won't slay people, people won't kill wolf, wolf won't eat goat, goat won't nibble bush, bush won't give little sparrow a swing.'

'I won't!' said the hen, 'but go to the sparrowhawk; he ought to give the first push, or why is he called the Pusher!'

So, the sparrow went to the sparrowhawk and said, 'Come, pusher, seize hen, hen won't peck worms, worms won't gnaw poleaxe, poleaxe won't strike ox, ox won't drink water, water won't quench fire, fire won't burn Tartars, Tartars won't slay people, people won't kill wolf, wolf won't eat goat, goat won't nibble bush, bush won't give little sparrow a swing.'

Then the sparrowhawk began to seize the hen, the hen began to peck the worms, the worms began to gnaw the poleaxe, the poleaxe began to hit the ox, the ox began to drink the water, the water began to quench the fire, the fire began to burn the Tartars, the Tartars began to slay the people, the people began to kill the wolf, the wolf began to eat the goat, the goat began to nibble the bush, and the bush cried out:

'*Swing away, swing away, swi-i-i-ing! Little daddy sparrow, have your fli-i-i-ing!*'

From: Cossack Folk Tales

The Princess on the Glass Hill

ONCE ON A time there was a man who had a meadow which lay high up on the hillside, and in the meadow was a barn, which he had built to keep his hay in.

Now, I must tell you, there hadn't been much in the barn for the last year or two, for every St. John's night, when the grass stood greenest and deepest, the meadow was eaten down to the very ground the next morning, just as if a whole drove of sheep had been there feeding on it overnight.

This happened once, and it happened twice; so at last, the man grew weary of losing his crop of hay, and said to his sons – for he had three of them, and the youngest was nicknamed *Boots*, of course – that now one of them must go and sleep in the barn in the outlying field when St. John's night came, for it was too good a joke that his grass should be eaten, root and blade, this year, as it had been the last two years. So whichever of them went must keep a sharp look-out; that was what their father said.

Well, the eldest son was ready to go and watch the meadow; trust him for looking after the grass! It shouldn't be his fault if man or beast, or the fiend himself, got a blade of grass. So, when evening came, he set off to the barn, and lay down to sleep; but a little on in the night came such a clatter, and such an earthquake, that walls and roof shook, and groaned, and creaked; then up jumped the lad, and took to his heels as fast as ever he could; nor dared he once look round till he reached home; and as for the hay, why it was eaten up this year just as it had been twice before.

The next St. John's night, the man said again, it would never do to lose all the grass in the outlying field year after year in this way, so one of his sons must just trudge off to watch it and watch it well, too. Well, the next oldest son was ready to try his luck, so he set off, and lay down to sleep in the barn as his brother had done before him; but as the night wore on, there came on a rumbling and quaking of the earth, worse even than on the last St. John's night, and when the lad heard it, he got frightened, and took to his heels as though he were running a race.

Next year, the turn came to *Boots*; but when he made ready to go, the other two began to laugh and to make game of him, saying: 'You're just the man to watch the hay, that you are; you, who have done nothing all your life but sit in the ashes and toast yourself by the fire.'

But *Boots* did not care a pin for their chattering, and stumped away as evening grew on, up the hillside to the outlying field. There he went inside the barn and lay down; but in about an hour's time the barn began to groan and creak, so that it was dreadful to hear.

'Well,' said *Boots* to himself, 'if it isn't worse than this, I can stand it well enough.'

A little while after came another creak and an earthquake, so that the litter in the barn flew about the lad's ears.

'Oh!' said *Boots* to himself, 'if it isn't worse than this, I daresay I can stand it out.'

But just then came a third rumbling, and a third earthquake, so that the lad thought walls and roof were coming down on his head; but it passed off, and all was still as death about him.

'It'll come again, I'll be bound,' thought *Boots*; but no, it didn't come again; still it was, and still it stayed; but after he had lain a little while, he heard a noise as if a horse were standing just outside the barn-door and cropping the grass. He stole to the door, and peeped through a chink, and there stood a horse feeding away. So big, and fat, and grand a horse, *Boots* had never set eyes on; by his side on the grass lay a saddle and bridle, and a full set of armour for a knight, all of brass, so bright that the light gleamed from it.

'Ho, ho!' thought the lad; 'it's you, is it, that eats up our hay? I'll soon put a spoke in your wheel, just see if I don't.'

So, he lost no time, but took the steel out of his tinder-box, and threw it over the horse; then it had no power to stir from the spot, and became so tame that the lad could do what he liked with it. So, he got on its back, and rode off with it to a place which no one knew of, and there he put up the horse. When he got home, his brothers laughed and asked how he had fared?

'You didn't lie long in the barn, even if you had the heart to go so far as the field.'

'Well,' said *Boots*, 'all I can say is, I lay in the barn till the sun rose, and neither saw nor heard anything; I can't think what there was in the barn to make you both so afraid.'

'A pretty story,' said his brothers; 'but we'll soon see how you have watched the meadow;' so they set off; but when they reached it, there stood the grass as deep and thick as it had been over night.

Well, the next St. John's eve it was the same story over again; neither of the elder brothers dared to go out to the outlying field to watch the crop; but *Boots*, he had the heart to go, and everything happened just as it had happened the year before. First a clatter and an earthquake, then a greater clatter and another earthquake, and so on a third time; only this year the earthquakes were far worse than the year before.

Then all at once everything was as still as death, and the lad heard how something was cropping the grass outside the barn-door, so he stole to the door, and peeped through a chink; and what do you think he saw? Why, another horse standing right up against the wall, and chewing and champing with might and main. It was far finer and fatter than that which came the year before, and it had a saddle on its back, and a bridle on its neck, and a full suit of mail for a knight lay by its side, all of silver, and as grand as you would wish to see.

'Ho, ho!' said *Boots* to himself; 'it's you that gobbles up our hay, is it? I'll soon put a spoke in your wheel;' and with that he took the steel out of his tinder-box, and threw it over the horse's crest, which stood as still as a lamb. Well, the lad rode this horse, too, to the hiding-place where he kept the other one, and after that he went home.

'I suppose you'll tell us,' said one of his brothers, 'there's a fine crop this year too, up in the hayfield.'

'Well, so there is,' said *Boots*; and off ran the others to see, and there stood the grass thick and deep, as it was the year before; but they didn't give *Boots* softer words for all that.

Now, when the third St. John's eve came, the two elder brothers still hadn't the heart to lie out in the barn and watch the grass, for they had got so scared at heart the nights they lay there before, that they couldn't get over the fright; but *Boots*, he dared to go; and, to make a very long story short, the very same thing happened this time as had happened twice before.

Three earthquakes came, one after the other, each worse than the one which went before, and when the last came, the lad danced about with the shock from one barn wall to the other; and after that, all at once, it was still as death. Now when he had laid a little while, he heard something tugging away at the grass outside the barn, so he stole again to the door-chink, and peeped out, and there stood a horse close outside – far, far bigger and fatter than the two he had taken before.

'Ho, ho!' said the lad to himself, 'it's you, is it, that comes here eating up our hay? I'll soon stop that – I'll soon put a spoke in your wheel.'

So, he caught up his steel and threw it over his horse's neck, and in a trice it stood as if it were nailed to the ground, and *Boots* could do as he pleased with it. Then he rode off with it to the hiding-place where he kept the other two, and then went home.

When he got home, his two brothers made game of him as they had done before, saying they could see he had watched the grass well, for he looked for all the world as if he were walking in his sleep, and many other spiteful things they said, but *Boots* gave no heed to them, only asking them to go and see for themselves; and when they went, there stood the grass as fine and deep this time as it had been twice before.

Now, you must know that the king of the country where *Boots* lived had a daughter, whom he would only give to the man who could ride up over the hill of glass, for there was a high, high hill, all of glass, as smooth and slippery as ice, close by the *prince's* palace.

Upon the tip top of the hill the *prince's* daughter was to sit, with three golden apples in her lap, and the man who could ride up and carry off the three golden apples, was to have half the kingdom, and the *princess* to wife.

This the *prince* had stuck up on all the church-doors in his realm and had given it out in many other kingdoms besides. Now, this *princess* was so lovely that all who set eyes on her fell over head and ears in love with her whether they would or no. So I needn't tell you how all the princes and knights who heard of her were eager to win her to wife, and half the kingdom beside; and how they came riding from all parts of the world on high prancing horses, and clad in the grandest clothes, for there wasn't one of them who hadn't made up his mind that he, and he alone, was to win the *princess*.

So when the day of trial came, which the king had fixed, there was such a crowd of princes and knights under the *Glass Hill*, that it made one's head whirl to look at them, and everyone in the country who could even crawl along was off to the hill, for they were all eager to see the man who was to win the *princess*. So, the two elder brothers set off with the rest; but as for *Boots*, they said outright he shouldn't go with them, for if they were seen with such a dirty changeling, all begrimed with smut from cleaning their shoes and sifting cinders in the dust-hole, they said folk would make game of them.

'Very well,' said *Boots*, 'it's all one to me. I can go alone and stand or fall by myself.'

Now when the two brothers came to the *Hill of Glass*, the knights and princes were all hard at it, riding their horses till they were all in a foam; but it was no good, by my troth; for as soon as ever the horses set foot on the hill, down they slipped, and there wasn't one who could get a yard or two up; and no wonder, for the hill was as smooth as a sheet of glass, and as steep as a house-wall. But all were eager to have the *princess* and half the kingdom.

So, they rode and slipped, and slipped and rode, and still it was the same story over again.

At last, all their horses were so weary that they could scarce lift a leg, and in such a sweat that the lather dripped from them, and so the knights had to give up trying any more. So the king was just thinking that he would proclaim a new trial for the next day, to see if they would have better luck, when all at once a knight came riding up on so brave a steed, that no one had ever seen the like of it in his born days, and the knight had mail of brass, and the horse a brass bit in his mouth, so bright that the sunbeams shone from it.

Then all the others called out to him he might just as well spare himself the trouble of riding at the Hill, for it would lead to no good; but he gave no heed to them, and put his horse at the hill, and went up it like nothing for a good way, about a third of the height; and when he had got so far, he turned his horse round and rode down again.

So lovely a knight the *princess* thought she had never yet seen; and while he was riding, she sat and thought to herself: 'Would to heaven he might only come up and down the other side.'

And when she saw him turning back, she threw down one of the golden apples after him, and it rolled down into his shoe. But when he got to the bottom of the hill, he rode off so fast that no one could tell what had become of him.

That evening, all the knights and princes were to go before the king, that he who had ridden so far up the hill might show the apple which the *princess* had thrown, but there was no one who had anything to show. One after the other they all came, but not a man of them could show the apple.

And even the brothers of *Boots* came home, too, and had such a long story to tell about the riding up the hill.

'First of all,' they said, 'there was not one of the whole lot who could get so much as a stride up; but at last came one who had a suit of brass mail, and a brass bridle and saddle, all so bright that the sun shone from them a mile off. He was a chap to ride, just! He rode a third of the way up the *Hill of Glass*, and he could easily have ridden the whole way up, if he chose; but he turned round and rode down, thinking, maybe, that was enough for once.'

'Oh! I should so like to have seen him, that I should,' said *Boots*, who sat by the fireside, and stuck his feet into the cinders, as was his wont.

'Oh!' said his brothers, 'you would, would you? You look fit to keep company with such high lords, nasty beast that you are, sitting there amongst the ashes.'

Next day, the brothers were all for setting off again, and *Boots* begged them this time, too, to let him go with them and see the riding; but no, they wouldn't have him at any price, he was too ugly and nasty, they said.

'Well, well!' said *Boots*; 'if I go at all, I must go by myself. I'm not afraid.'

So when the brothers got to the *Hill of Glass*, all the princes and knights began to ride again, and you may fancy they had taken care to shoe their horses sharp; but it was no good –they rode and slipped, and slipped and rode, just as they had done the day before, and there was not one who could get so far as a yard up the hill.

And when they had worn out their horses, so that they could not stir a leg, they were all forced to give it up as a bad job. So, the king thought he might as well proclaim that the riding should take place the day after for the last time, just to give them one chance more; but all at once it came across his mind that he might as well wait a little longer, to see if the knight in brass mail would come this day too.

Well, they saw nothing of him; but all at once came one riding on a steed, far, far braver and finer than that on which the knight in brass had ridden, and he had silver mail, and a silver saddle and bridle, all so bright that the sunbeams gleamed and glanced from them far away.

Then the others shouted out to him again, saying, he might as well hold hard, and not try to ride up the hill, for all his trouble would be thrown away; but the knight paid no heed to them, and rode straight at the hill, and right up it, till he had gone two-thirds of the way, and then he wheeled his horse round and rode down again.

To tell the truth, the *princess* liked him still better than the knight in brass, and she sat and wished he might only be able to come right up to the top, and down the other side; but when she saw him turning back, she threw the second apple after him, and it rolled down and fell into his shoe. But, as soon as ever he had come down from the *Hill of Glass*, he rode off so fast that no one could see what became of him.

At even, when all were to go in before the king and the *princess*, that he who had the golden apple might show it, in they went, one after the other, but there was no one who had any apple to show, and the two brothers, as they had done on the former day, went home and told how things had gone, and how all had ridden at the hill, and none got up.

'But, last of all,' they said, 'came one in a silver suit, and his horse had a silver saddle and a silver bridle. He was just a chap to ride; and he got two-thirds up the hill, and then turned back. He was a fine fellow, and no mistake; and the *princess* threw the second gold apple to him.'

'Oh!' said *Boots*, 'I should so like to have seen him too, that I should.'

'A pretty story,' they said. 'Perhaps you think his coat of mail was as bright as the ashes you are always poking about, and sifting, you nasty dirty beast.'

The third day everything happened as it had happened the two days before. Boots begged to go and see the sight, but the two wouldn't hear of his going with them. When they got to the hill, there was no one who could get so much as a yard up it; and now all waited for the knight in silver mail, but they neither saw nor heard of him. At last came one riding on a steed, so brave that no one had ever seen his match; and the knight had a suit of golden mail, and a golden saddle and bridle, so wondrous bright that the sunbeams gleamed from them a mile off.

The other knights and princes could not find time to call out to him not to try his luck, for they were amazed to see how grand he was. So, he rode right at the hill, and tore up it like nothing, so that the *princess* hadn't even time to wish that he might get up the whole way. As soon as ever he reached the top, he took the third golden apple from the *princess'* lap, and then turned his horse and rode down again. As soon as he got down, he rode off at full speed, and was out of sight in no time.

Now, when the brothers got home at even, you may fancy what long stories they told, how the riding had gone off that day; and amongst other things, they had a deal to say about the knight in golden mail.

'He just was a chap to ride!' they said, 'so grand a knight isn't to be found in the wide world.'

'Oh!' said *Boots*, 'I should so like to have seen him, that I should.'

'Ah!' said his brothers, 'his mail shone a deal brighter than the glowing coals which you are always poking and digging at; nasty dirty beast that you are.'

Next day, all the knights and princes were to pass before the king and the *princess* – it was too late to do so the night before, I suppose – that he who had the gold apple might bring it forth; but one came after another, first the *princes*, and then the knights, and still no one could show the gold apple.

'Well,' said the king, 'someone must have it, for it was something we all saw with our own eyes, how a man came and rode up and bore it off.'

So, he commanded that every man who was in the kingdom should come up to the palace and see if they could show the apple. Well, they all came one after another, but no one had the golden apple, and after a long time the two brothers of *Boots* came. They were the last of all, so the king asked them if there was no one else in the kingdom who hadn't come.

'Oh, yes,' said they; 'we have a brother, but he never carried off the golden apple. He hasn't stirred out of the dust-hole on any of the three days.'

'Never mind that,' said the king; 'he may as well come up to the palace like the rest.'

So, *Boots* had to go up to the palace.

'How now,' said the king; 'have you got the golden apple? Speak out!'

'Yes, I have,' said *Boots*; 'here is the first, and here is the second, and here is the third too;' and with that he pulled all three golden apples out of his pocket, and at the same time threw off his sooty rags and stood before them in his gleaming golden mail.

'Yes!' said the king; 'you shall have my daughter, and half my kingdom, for you well deserve both her and it.'

So they got ready for the wedding, and *Boots* got the *princess* to wife, and there was great merry-making at the bridal-feast, you may fancy, for they could all be merry though they couldn't ride up the *Hill of Glass*; and all I can say is, if they haven't left off their merry-making yet, why, they're still at it.

From: East of the Sun & West of the Moon

The Sea Moans

ONCE UPON A time, there was a little princess who lived in a magnificent royal palace.

All around the palace there was a beautiful garden full of lovely flowers and rare shrubs and trees. The part of the garden which the princess liked most of all was a corner of it which ran down to the sea.

She was a very lonely little princess and she loved to sit and watch the changing beauty of the sea. The name of the little princess was Dionysia and it often seemed to her that the sea said, as it rushed against the shore, 'Di-o-ny-si-a, Di-o-ny-si-a.'

One day when the little princess was sitting all alone by the sea, she said to herself, 'O! I am so lonely. I do so wish that I had somebody to play with. When I ride out in the royal chariot, I see little girls who have other little boys and girls to play with them. Because I am the royal princess, I never have anybody to play with me. If I have to be the royal princess and not play with other children, I do think I might have some sort of live thing to play with me.'

Then a most remarkable thing happened. The sea said very slowly and distinctly and over and over again so there couldn't be any mistake about it, 'Di-o-ny-si-a, Di-o-ny-si-a.'

The little princess walked up close to the sea, just as close as she dared to go without danger of getting her royal shoes and stockings wet. Straight out of the biggest wave of all there came a sea serpent to meet her. She knew that it was a sea serpent from the pictures in her royal story books, even though she had never seen a sea serpent before, but somehow this sea serpent looked different than the pictures. Instead of being a fierce monster it looked kind and gentle and good. She held out her arms to it right away.

'Come play with me,' said Dionysia.

'I am Labismena and I have come to play with you,' replied the sea serpent.

After that, the little princess was very much happier. The sea serpent came out of the sea to play with her every day when she was alone. If anyone else came near, Labismena would disappear into the sea so no one but Dionysia ever saw her.

The years passed rapidly and each year the little princess grew to be a larger and larger princess. At last, she was sixteen years old and a very grown-up princess indeed. She still enjoyed her old playmate, Labismena, and they were often together on the seashore.

One day when they were walking up and down together beside the sea the sea serpent looked at Dionysia with sad eyes and said, 'I too have been growing older all these years, dear Dionysia. Now the time has come that we can no longer play together. I shall never come out of the sea to play with you anymore, but I shall never forget you and I shall always be your friend. I hope that you will never have any trouble, but if you ever should, call my name and I will come to help you.'

Then the sea serpent disappeared into the sea.

About this time the wife of a neighbouring king died and as she lay upon her deathbed, she gave the king a jewelled ring.

'When the time comes when you wish to wed again,' she said, 'I ask you to marry a princess upon whose finger this ring shall be neither too tight nor too loose.'

After a while, the king began to look about for a princess to be his bride. He visited many royal palaces and tried the ring upon the finger of many royal princesses. Upon some the ring was too tight and upon others it was too loose. There was no princess whose finger it fitted perfectly.

At last, in his search the king came to the royal palace where the princess Dionysia lived. The princess had dreams of her own of a young and charming prince who would someday come to wed her, so she was not pleased at all. The king was old and no longer handsome, and when he tried the ring upon Dionysia's finger, she hoped with all her heart that it would not fit.

It fitted perfectly.

The princess Dionysia was frightened nearly to death.

'Will I really have to marry him?' she asked her royal father.

Her father told her what a very wealthy king he was with a great kingdom and a wonderful royal palace ever so much more wonderful and grand than the palace the princess Dionysia had always had for her home. Her father had no patience at all with her for not being happy about it.

'You ought to consider yourself the most fortunate princess in all the world,' he said.

Dionysia spent her days and nights weeping. Her father was afraid that she would grow so thin that the ring would no longer fit her finger, so he hastened the plans for the wedding.

One day Dionysia walked up and down beside the sea, crying as if her heart would break. All at once she stopped crying.

'How stupid I have been,' she said. 'My old playmate Labismena told me that if ever I was in trouble she would come back and help me. With all my silly crying I had forgotten about it.'

Dionysia walked up close to the sea and called softly, 'Labismena, Labismena.'

Out of the sea came the sea serpent just as she used to come. The princess told the sea serpent all about the dreadful trouble which was threatening to spoil her life.

'Have no fear,' said Labismena, 'tell your father that you will marry the king when the king presents you with a dress the colour of the fields and all their flowers and that you will not marry him until he gives it to you.' Then the sea serpent disappeared again into the sea.

Dionysia sent word through her father to her royal suitor that she would wed him only when he procured her a dress the colour of the fields and all their flowers. The king was very much in love with Dionysia, so he was secretly filled with joy at this request. He searched everywhere for a dress the colour of the fields and all their flowers. It was a very difficult thing to find but at last he procured one. He sent it to Dionysia at once.

When Dionysia saw that the king had really found the dress for her, she was filled with grief. She thought that there was no escape and that she would have to marry the king after all. As soon as she could get away from the palace without being noticed she ran down to the sea and again called, 'Labismena, Labismena.'

The sea serpent at once came out of the sea.

'Do not fear,' she said to Dionysia. 'Go back and say that you will not wed the king until he gives you a dress the colour of the sea and all its fishes.'

When the king heard this new request of Dionysia's he was rather discouraged.

However, he searched for the dress and, at last, after expending a great sum of money, he procured such a gown.

When Dionysia saw that a dress the colour of the sea and all its fishes had been found for her, she again went to seek counsel from her old playmate.

'Do not be afraid,' Labismena again said to her. 'This time you must ask the king to get you a dress the colour of the sky and all its stars. You may also tell him that this is the last present you will ask him to make you.'

When the king heard about the demand for a dress the colour of the sky and all its stars he was completely disheartened, but when he heard that Dionysia had promised that this would be the last present she would ask, he decided that it might be a good investment after all. He set out to procure the dress with all possible speed.

At last, he found one.

When Dionysia saw the dress the colour of the sky and all its stars, she thought that this time there was no escape from marrying the king. She called the sea serpent with an anxious heart for she was afraid that now even Labismena could do nothing to help her.

Labismena came out of the sea in answer to her call.

'Go home to the palace and get your dress the colour of the field and all its flowers,' said the sea serpent, 'and your dress the colour of the sea and all its fishes, and your dress the colour of the sky and all its stars. Then hurry back here to the sea, for I have been preparing a surprise for you.'

All the time the king had been procuring the wonderful gowns for Dionysia, the sea serpent had been building a ship for her. When Dionysia returned from the royal palace with her lovely dresses all carefully packed in a box there was a queer little boat awaiting her. It was not at all like any other boat she had ever seen, and she was almost afraid to get into it when Labismena asked her to try it.

'This little ship which I have built for you,' said Labismena, 'will carry you far away over the sea to the kingdom of a prince who is the most charming prince in all the world. When you see him, you will want to marry him above all others.'

'O, Labismena! How can I ever thank you for all you have done for me?' cried Dionysia.

'You can do the greatest thing in the world for me,' said Labismena; 'though I have never told you and I do not believe that you have ever suspected it, I am really an enchanted princess. I shall have to remain in the form of a sea serpent until the happiest maiden in all the world, at the hour of her greatest happiness, calls my name three times. You will be the very happiest girl in all the world on the day of your marriage, and if you will remember to call my name three times then you will break my enchantment and I shall once more be a lovely princess instead of a sea serpent.'

Dionysia promised her friend that she would remember to do this. The sea serpent asked her to promise three times to make sure. When Dionysia had promised three times and again embraced her old playmate and thanked her for all that she had done she sailed away in the little ship. The sea serpent disappeared into the sea.

Dionysia sailed and sailed in the little ship and at last it bore her to a lovely island. She thought that she had reached her destination, so she stepped out of the boat, not forgetting to take her box of dresses with her. As soon as she was out of the boat, it sailed away.

'Now what shall I ever do?' said Dionysia. 'The ship has gone away and left me and how shall I ever earn my living? I have never done anything useful in all my life.'

Dionysia surely had to do something to earn her living immediately, so she at once set out to see what she could find to do. She went from house to house asking for food and work. At last, she came to the royal palace. Here at the royal palace, they told her that they had great need of a maid to take care of the hens. Dionysia thought that this was something which she could do, so she accepted the position at once. It was, of course, very different work from being a princess in a royal palace, but it provided her with food and shelter, and when Dionysia thought of having to marry the old king, she was never sorry that she had left home.

Time passed and at last there was a great feast day celebrated in the city. Everybody in the palace went except the little maid who minded the hens. After everybody had gone away Dionysia decided that she would go to the *festa* too. She combed her hair and put on her gown which was the colour of the fields and all their flowers. In this wonderful gown she was sure nobody would ever guess that she was the little maid who had been left at home to mind the hens. She did want to go to the *festa*! She hurried there as fast as she could and arrived just in time for the dances.

Everybody at the *festa* noticed the beautiful maiden in her gown the colour of the fields and all their flowers. The prince fell madly in love with her. Nobody had ever seen her before, and nobody could find out who the beautiful stranger was or where she came from. Before the *festa* was over Dionysia slipped away, and, when the rest of the royal household returned home there was the little maid minding the hens just as they had left her.

The second day of the *festa*, everybody went early except the little maid who looked after the hens. When the others had gone, she put on her dress the colour of the sea and all its fishes and went to the *festa*. She attracted even more attention than she had the day before.

When the *festa* was over and the royal household had returned to the royal palace, the prince remarked to his mother, 'Don't you think that the beautiful stranger at the *festa* looks like the little maid who minds our hens?'

'What nonsense,' replied his mother. 'How could the little maid who minds our hens ever get such wonderful gowns to wear?'

Just to make sure, however, the prince told the royal councillor to find out if the little maid who minds the royal hens had been to the *festa*. All the servants told about leaving her at home with the hens and coming back and finding her just as they had left her.

'Whoever the beautiful stranger at the *festa* may be,' said the prince, 'she is the one above all others whom I want for my wife. I shall find her some way.'

The third day of the *festa* Dionysia went attired in her gown the colour of the sky and all its stars. The prince fell more madly in love with her than ever. He could not get her to tell him who she was or where she lived but he gave her a beautiful jewel.

When the prince returned home, he would not eat any food. He grew thin and pale. Everyone around the palace tried his best to invent some dish which would tempt the prince's appetite.

Finally, the little maid who took care of the hens said that she thought she could prepare a dish which the prince would eat.

Accordingly, she made a dish of broth for the prince and in the bottom of the dish she dropped the jewel which the prince had given her.

When the broth was set before the prince, he was about to send it away untouched, just as he did everything else, but the sparkling jewel attracted his attention.

'Who made this dish of broth?' he asked as soon as he could speak.

'It was made by the little maid who minds the hens,' replied his mother.

'Send for the little maid to come to me at once,' cried the prince. 'I knew that the beautiful stranger at the *festa* looked like our little maid who minds the hens.'

The prince married Dionysia the very next day and Dionysia was the very happiest girl in all the world, for from the first moment that she had seen the prince, she had known that he was the one above all others whom she wished to marry.

Alas! In Dionysia's excitement she forgot all about calling the name of her old playmate, Labismena, at the hour of her marriage as she had promised to do. She thought of nothing but the prince.

There was no escape for Labismena. She had to remain in the form of a sea serpent because of Dionysia's neglect. She had lost her chance to come out of the sea and become a lovely princess herself and find a charming prince of her own. For this reason, her sad moan is heard in the sea until this very day. Perhaps you have noticed it.

You will often hear the call come from the sea as it breaks against the shore, 'Dionysia, Di-o-ny-si-a.'

No wonder that the sea moans. It is enough to make a sea serpent sad to be forgotten by the very person one has done most to help.

From: Fairy Tales from Brazil

The Perfidious Vizier

A KING OF former times had an only son, whom he contracted in marriage to the daughter of another king.

But the damsel, who was endowed with great beauty, had a cousin who had sought her in marriage, and had been rejected; wherefore he sent great presents to the vizier of the king just mentioned, requesting him to employ some stratagem by which to destroy his master's son, or to induce him to relinquish the damsel.

The vizier consented. Then the father of the damsel sent to the king's son, inviting him to come and introduce himself to his daughter, to take her as his wife; and the father of the young man sent him with the treacherous vizier, attended by a thousand horsemen, and provided with rich presents.

When they were proceeding over the desert, the vizier remembered that there was near unto them a spring of water called Ez-zahra, and that whosoever drank of it, if he were a man, became a woman. He therefore ordered the troops to alight near it and induced the prince to go thither with him.

When they arrived at the spring, the king's son dismounted from his courser, and washed his hands, and drank; and lo! He became a woman; whereupon he cried out and wept until he fainted. The vizier asked him what had befallen him, so the young man informed him; and on hearing his words, the vizier affected to be grieved for him, and wept. The king's son then sent the vizier back to his father to inform him of this event, determining not to proceed nor to return until his affliction should be removed from him, or until he should die.

He remained by the fountain during a period of three days and nights, neither eating nor drinking, and on the fourth night there came to him a horseman with a crown upon his head, appearing like one of the sons of the kings.

This horseman said to him, 'Who brought you, O young man, unto this place?'

So, the young man told him his story; and when the horseman heard it, he pitied him, and said to him, 'The vizier of your father is the person who has thrown you into this calamity; for no one of mankind knows of this spring excepting one man.'

Then the horseman ordered him to mount with him. He therefore mounted; and the horseman said to him, 'Come with me to my abode: for you are my guest this night.'

The young man replied, 'Inform me who you are before I go with you.'

And the horseman said, 'I am the son of a king of the jinn, and you are son of a king of mankind. And now, be of good heart and cheerful eye on account of that which shall dispel your anxiety and your grief, for it is unto me easy.'

So, the young man proceeded with him from the commencement of the day, forsaking his troops and soldiers (whom the vizier had left at their halting-place), and ceased not to travel on with his conductor until midnight, when the son of the king of the jinn said to him, 'Know you what space we have traversed during this period?'

The young man answered him, 'I know not.'

The son of the king of the jinn said, 'We have traversed a space of a year's journey to him who travells with diligence.'

So, the young man wondered thereat, and asked, 'How shall I return to my family?'

The other answered, 'This is not your affair. It is my affair; and when you shall have recovered from your misfortune, you shall return to your family in less time than the twinkling of an eye, for to accomplish that will be to me easy.'

The young man, on hearing these words from the jinn, almost flew with excessive delight. He thought that the event was a result of confused dreams, and said, 'Extolled be the perfection of him who is able to restore the wretched, and render him prosperous!'

They ceased not to proceed until morning, when they arrived at a verdant, bright land, with tall trees, and warbling birds, and gardens of surpassing beauty, and fair palaces; and thereupon the son of the king of the jinn alighted from his courser, commanding the young man also to dismount.

He therefore dismounted, and the jinn took him by the hand, and they entered one of the palaces, where the young man beheld an exalted king and a sultan of great dignity, and he remained with them that day, eating and drinking, until the approach of night.

Then the son of the king of the jinn arose and mounted with him, and they went forth, and proceeded during the night with diligence until the morning. And lo! They came to a black land, not inhabited, abounding with black rocks and stones, as though it were a part of hell; whereupon the son of the king of men said to the jinn, 'What is the name of this land?'

And he answered, 'It is called the Dusky Land, and it belongs to one of the kings of the jinn, whose name is Zu-l-Jenáheyn. None of the kings can attack him, nor doe anyone enter his territory unless by his permission, so stop in your place while I ask his permission.'

Accordingly, the young man stopped, and the jinn was absent from him for a while, and then returned to him; and they ceased not to proceed until they came to a spring flowing from black mountains.

The jinn spoke a single word to the young man: 'Alight.'

He therefore alighted from his courser, and the jinn said to him, 'Drink of this spring.'

The young prince drank of it, and immediately became again a man, as he was at first, by the power of God (whose name be exalted!), whereat he rejoiced with great joy, not to be exceeded.

And he said to the jinn, 'O my brother, what is the name of this spring?'

The jinn answered, 'It is called the Spring of the Women: no woman drinks of it but she becomes a man; therefore, praise God, and thank Him for your restoration, and mount your courser.'

So, the king's son prostrated himself, thanking God (whose name be exalted!).

Then he mounted, and they journeyed with diligence during the rest of the day until they had returned to the land of the jinn, and the young man passed the night in his abode in the most comfortable manner; after which they ate and drank until the next night, when the son of the king of the jinn said to him, 'Do you desire to return to your family this night?'

The young man answered, 'Yes.'

So, the son of the king of the jinn called one of his father's slaves, whose name was Rájiz, and said to him, 'Take this young man hence, and carry him upon your shoulders, and let not the dawn overtake him before he is with his father-in-law and his wife.'

The slave replied, 'I hear and obey, and with feelings of love and honour will I do it.'

Then the slave absented himself for a while and approached in the form of an efreet. And when the young man saw him, his reason fled, and he was stupefied; but the son of the king of the jinn said to him, 'No harm shall befall you. Mount your courser. Ascend upon his shoulders.'

The young man then mounted upon the slave's shoulders, and the son of the king of the jinn said to him, 'Close your eyes.'

So, he closed his eyes, and the slave flew with him between heaven and earth, and ceased not to fly along with him while the young man was unconscious, and the last third of the night came not before he was on the top of the palace of his father-in-law.

Then the efreet said to him, 'Alight.'

He therefore alighted.

And the efreet said to him, 'Open your eyes; for this is the palace of your father-in-law and his daughter.'

Then he left him and departed. And as soon as the day shone, and the alarm of the young man subsided, he descended from the roof of the palace; and when his father-in-law beheld him, he rose to him and met him, wondering at seeing him descend from the top of the palace, and he said to him,

'We see other men come through the doors, but you come down from the sky.'

The young man replied, 'What God (whose perfection be extolled, and whose name be exalted!) desired has happened.'

And when the sun rose, his father-in-law ordered his vizier to prepare great banquets, and the wedding was celebrated; the young man remained there two months, and then departed with his wife to the city of his father.

But as to the cousin of the damsel, he perished by reason of his jealousy and envy.

From: Oriental Folklore & Legends

The Bird-lover

IN A REGION of country where the forest and the prairie strived which should be the most beautiful – the open plain, with its free sunshine and winds and flowers, or the close wood, with its delicious twilight-walks and enamoured haunts – there lived a wicked manito in the disguise of an old Indian.

Although the country furnished an abundance of game, and whatever else a good heart could wish for, it was the study of this wicked genius to destroy such as fell into his hands. He made use of all his arts to decoy men into his power, for the purpose of killing them. The country had been once thickly peopled, but this Mudjee Monedo had so thinned it by his cruel practices, that he now lived almost solitary in the wilderness.

The secret of his success lay in his great speed. He had the power to assume the shape of any four-footed creature, and it was his custom to challenge such as he sought to destroy, to run with him. He had a beaten path on which he ran, leading around a large lake, and he always ran around this circle so that the starting and the winning post was the same.

Whoever failed as everyone had, yielded up his life at this post; and although he ran every day, no man was ever known to beat this evil genius; for whenever he was pressed hard, he changed himself into a fox, wolf, deer, or other swift-footed animal, and was thus able to leave his competitor behind.

The whole country was in dread of this same Mudjee Monedo, and yet the young men were constantly running with him; for if they refused, he called them cowards, which was a reproach they could not bear. They would rather die than be called cowards.

To keep up his sport, the manito made light of these deadly foot-matches, and instead of assuming a braggart air, and going about in a boastful way, with the blood of such as he had overcome, upon his hands, he adopted very pleasing manners, and visited the lodges around the country as any other sweet-tempered and harmless old Indian might.

His secret object in these friendly visits was to learn whether the young boys were getting old enough to run with him; he kept a very sharp eye upon their growth, and the day he thought them ready, he did not fail to challenge them to a trial on his racing-ground.

There was not a family in all that beautiful region which had not in this way been visited and thinned out; and the manito had quite naturally come to be held in abhorrence by all the Indian mothers in the country.

It happened that there lived near him a poor widow woman whose husband and seven sons he had made way with; and she was now living with an only daughter and a son of ten or twelve years old.

This widow was very poor and feeble, and she suffered so much for lack of food and other comforts of the lodge that she would have been glad to die, but for her daughter and her little son. The Mudjee Monedo had already visited her lodge to observe whether the boy was sufficiently grown to be challenged to the race; and so crafty in his approaches and so soft in his manners was the monedo, that the mother feared that he would yet decoy the son and make way with him as he had done with his father and his seven brothers, in spite of all her struggles to save him.

And yet, she strove with all her might to strengthen her son in every good course. She taught him, as best she could, what was becoming for the wise hunter and the brave warrior. She remembered and set before him all that she could recall of the skill and the craft of his father and his brothers who were lost.

The widow woman also instructed her daughter in whatever could make her useful as a wife; and in the leisure-time of the lodge, she gave her lessons in the art of working with the quills of porcupine, and bestowed on her such other accomplishments as should make her an ornament and a blessing to her husband's household. The daughter, Minda by name, was kind and obedient to her mother, and never failed in her duty. Their lodge stood high up on the banks of a lake, which gave them a wide prospect of country, embellished with groves and open fields, which waved with the blue light of their long grass, and made, at all hours of sun and moon, a cheerful scene to look upon.

Across this beautiful prairie, Minda had one morning made her way to gather dry limbs for their fire; for she disdained no labour of the lodge. And while enjoying the sweetness of the air and the green beauty of the woods, she strolled far away.

She had come to a bank, painted with flowers of every hue, and was reclining on its fragrant couch when a bird, of red and deep-blue plumage softly blended, alighted on a branch nearby, and began to pour forth its carol. It was a bird of strange character, such as she had never before seen. Its first note was so delicious to the ear of Minda, and it so pierced to her young heart, that she listened as she had never before to any mortal or heavenly sound. It seemed like the human voice, forbidden to speak, and uttering its language through this wild wood-chant with a mournful melody, as if it bewailed the lack of the power or the right to make itself more plainly intelligible.

The voice of the bird rose and fell, and circled round and round, but whithersoever floated or spread out its notes, they seemed ever to have their centre where Minda sat; and she looked with sad eyes into the sad eyes of the mournful bird, that sat in his red and deep-blue plumage just opposite to the flowery bank.

The poor bird strove more and more with his voice, and seemed ever more and more anxiously to address his notes of lament to Minda's ear, till at last she could not refrain from saying, 'What ails you, sad bird?'

As if he had but waited to be spoken to, the bird left his branch, and alighting upon the bank, smiled on Minda, and, shaking his shining plumage, answered: 'I am bound in this condition until a maiden shall accept me in marriage. I have wandered these groves and sung to many and many of the Indian girls, but none ever heeded my voice till you. Will you be mine?' he added and poured forth a flood of melody which sparkled and spread itself with its sweet murmurs over all the scene, and fairly entranced the young Minda, who sat silent, as if she feared to break the charm by speech.

The bird, approaching nearer, asked her, if she loved him, to get her mother's consent to their marriage.

'I shall be free then,' said the bird, 'and you shall know me as I am.'

Minda lingered, and listened to the sweet voice of the bird in its own forest notes, or filling each pause with gentle human discourse, questioning her as to her home, her family, and the little incidents of her daily life.

She returned to the lodge later than usual, but she was too timid to speak to her mother of that which the bird had charged her. She returned again and again to the fragrant haunt in the wood; and every day she listened to the song and the discourse of her bird admirer with more pleasure, and he every day besought her to speak to her mother of the marriage. This she could not, however, muster heart and courage to do.

At last, the widow began herself to have a suspicion that her daughter's heart was in the wood, from her long delays in returning, and the little success she had in gathering the fire-branches for which she went in search.

In answer to her mother's questions, Minda revealed the truth, and made known her lover's request. The mother, considering the lonely and destitute condition of her little household, gave her consent.

The daughter, with light steps, hastened with the news to the wood. The bird lover of course heard it with delight, and fluttered through the air in happy circles, and poured forth a song of joy which thrilled Minda to the heart.

He said that he would come to the lodge at sunset, and immediately took wing, while Minda hung fondly upon his flight, till he was lost far away in the blue sky.

With the twilight, the bird lover, whose name was Monedowa, appeared at the door of the lodge as a hunter, with a red plume and a mantle of blue upon his shoulders.

He addressed the widow as his friend, and she directed him to sit down beside her daughter, and they were regarded as man and wife.

Early on the following morning, he asked for the bow and arrows of those who had been slain by the wicked manito and went out a-hunting. As soon as he had got out of sight of the lodge, he changed himself into the wood-bird, as he had been before his marriage, and took his flight through the air.

Although game was scarce in the neighbourhood of the widow's lodge, Monedowa returned at evening in his character of a hunter, with two deer. This was his daily practice, and the widow's family never more lacked for food.

It was noticed, however, that Monedowa himself ate but little, and that of a peculiar kind of meat, flavoured with berries, which, with other circumstances, convinced them that he was not as the Indian people around him.

In a few days, his mother-in-law told him that the manito would come to pay them a visit to see how the young man, her son, prospered.

Monedowa answered that he should on that day be absent. When the time arrived, he flew upon a tall tree, overlooking the lodge, and took his station there as the wicked manito passed in.

The Mudjee Monedo cast sharp glances at the scaffolds so well laden with meat, and as soon as he had entered, he said, 'Why, who is it that is furnishing you with meat so plentifully?'

'No one,' she answered, 'but my son; he is just beginning to kill deer.'

'No, no,' he retorted; 'someone is living with you.'

'Kaween, no indeed,' replied the widow; 'you are only making sport of my hapless condition. Who do you think would come and trouble themselves about me?'

'Very well,' answered the manito, 'I will go; but on such a day I will again visit you, and see who it is that furnishes the meat, and whether it is your son or not.'

He had no sooner left the lodge and got out of sight, than the son-in-law made his appearance with two more deer. On being made acquainted with the conduct of the manito,

'Very well,' he said, 'I will be at home the next time, to see him.'

Both the mother and the wife urged Monedowa to be aware of the manito. They made known to him all of his cruel courses and assured him that no man could escape from his power.

'No matter,' said Monedowa; 'if he invites me to the race-ground, I will not be backward. What follows may teach him, my mother, to show pity on the vanquished, and not to trample on the widow and those who are without fathers.'

When the day of the visit of the manito arrived, Monedowa told his wife to prepare certain pieces of meat, which he pointed out to her, together with two or three buds of the birch-tree, which he requested her to put in the pot. He directed also that the manito should be hospitably received, as if he had been just the kind-hearted old Indian he professed to be. Monedowa then dressed himself as a warrior, embellishing his visage with tints of red, to show that he was prepared for either war or peace.

As soon as the Mudjee Monedo arrived, he eyed this strange warrior whom he had never seen before; but he dissembled, as usual, and, with a gentle laugh, said to the widow, 'Did I not tell you that someone was staying with you, for I knew your son was too young to hunt.'

The widow excused herself by saying that she did not think it necessary to tell him, inasmuch as he was a manito, and must have known before he asked.

The manito was very pleasant with Monedowa, and after much other discourse, in a gentle-spoken voice, he invited him to the racing-ground, saying it was a manly amusement, that he would have an excellent chance to meet there with other warriors, and that he should himself be pleased to run with him.

Monedowa would have excused himself, saying that he knew nothing of running.

'Why,' replied the Mudjee Monedo, trembling in every limb as he spoke, 'don't you see how old I look, while you are young and full of life. We must at least run a little to amuse others.'

'Be it so, then,' replied Monedowa. 'I will oblige you. I will go in the morning.'

Pleased with his crafty success, the manito would have now taken his leave, but he was pressed to remain and partake of their hospitality. The meal was immediately prepared. But one dish was used.

Monedowa partook of it first, to show his guest that he need not fear, saying at the same time, 'It is a feast, and as we seldom meet, we must eat all that is placed on the dish, as a mark of gratitude to the Great Spirit for permitting me to kill animals, and for the pleasure of seeing you, and partaking of it with you.'

They ate and talked on this and that, until they had nearly dispatched the meal, when the manito took up the dish and drank off the broth at a breath. On setting it down, he immediately turned his head and commenced coughing with great violence. The old body in which he had disguised himself was well-nigh shaken in pieces, for he had, as Monedowa expected, swallowed a grain of the birch-bud, and this, which relished to himself as being of the bird nature, greatly distressed the old manito, who partook of the character of an animal, or four-footed thing.

He was at last put to such confusion of face by his constant coughing, that he was enforced to leave, saying, or rather hiccoughing as he left the lodge, that he should look for the young man at the racing-ground in the morning.

When the morning came, Monedowa was early astir, oiling his limbs and enamelling his breast and arms with red and blue, resembling the plumage in which he had first appeared to Minda. Upon his brow he placed a tuft of feathers of the same shining tints.

By his invitation, his wife, Minda, the mother and her young son, attended Monedowa to the manito's racing-ground.

The lodge of the manito stood upon a high ground, and near it stretched out a long row of other lodges, said to be possessed by wicked kindred of his, who shared in the spoils of his cruelty.

As soon as the young hunter and his party approached, the inmates appeared at their lodge-doors and cried out: 'We are visited.'

At this cry, the Mudjee Monedo came forth and descended with his companions to the starting-post on the plain. From this, the course could be seen, winding in a long girdle about the lake; and as they were now all assembled, the old manito began to speak of the race, belted himself up and pointed to the post, which was an upright pillar of stone.

'But before we start,' said the manito, 'I wish it to be understood that when men run with me, I make a wager, and I expect them to abide by it – life against life.'

'Very well – be it so,' answered Monedowa. 'We shall see whose head is to be dashed against the stone.'

'We shall,' rejoined the mudjee monedo. 'I am very old, but I shall try and make a run.'

'Very well,' again rejoined Monedowa; 'I hope we shall both stand to our bargain.'

'Good!' said the old manito; and he at the same time cast a sly glance at the young hunter, and rolled his eyes toward where stood the pillar of stone.

'I am ready,' said Monedowa.

The starting shout was given, and they set off at high speed, the manito leading, and Monedowa pressing closely after. As he closed upon him, the old manito began to show his power, and changing himself into a fox he passed the young hunter with ease and went leisurely along.

Monedowa now, with a glance upward, took the shape of the strange bird of red and deep-blue plumage, and with one flight, lighting at some distance ahead of the manito, resumed his mortal shape.

When the Mudjee Monedo espied his competitor before him, 'Whoa! Whoa!' he exclaimed; 'this is strange;' and he immediately changed himself into a wolf and sped past Monedowa.

As he galloped by, Monedowa heard a noise from his throat, and he knew that he was still in distress from the birch-bud which he had swallowed at his mother-in-law's lodge.

Monedowa again took wing, and, shooting into the air, he descended suddenly with great swiftness, and took the path far ahead of the old manito.

As he passed the wolf he whispered in his ear: 'My friend, is this the extent of your speed?'

The manito began to be troubled with bad forebodings, for, on looking ahead, he saw the young hunter in his own manly form, running along at leisure. The Mudjee Monedo, seeing the necessity of more speed, now passed Monedowa in the shape of a deer.

They were now far around the circle of the lake, and fast closing in upon the starting-post, when Monedowa, putting on his red and blue plumage, glided along the air and alighted upon the track far in advance.

To overtake him, the old manito assumed the shape of the buffalo; and he pushed on with such long gallops that he was again the foremost on the course. The buffalo was the last change he could make, and it was in this form that he had most frequently conquered.

The young hunter, once more a bird, in the act of passing the manito, saw his tongue lolling from his mouth with fatigue.

'My friend,' said Monedowa, 'is this all your speed?'

The manito made no answer. Monedowa had resumed his character of a hunter and was within a run of the winning-post, when the wicked manito had nearly overtaken him.

'Bakah! Bakah! Nejee!' he called out to Monedowa; 'stop, my friend, I wish to talk to you.'

Monedowa laughed aloud as he replied: 'I will speak to you at the starting-post. When men run with me, I make a wager, and I expect them to abide by it – life against life.'

One more flight as the blue bird with red wings, and Monedowa was so near to the goal that he could easily reach it in his mortal shape. Shining in beauty, his face lighted up like the sky, with tinted arms and bosom gleaming in the sun, and the parti-coloured plume on his brow waving in the wind. Monedowa, cheered by a joyful shout from his own people, leaped to the post.

The manito came on with fear in his face. 'My friend,' he said, 'spare my life;' and then added, in a low voice, as if he would not that the others should hear it, 'Give me to live.'

And he began to move off as if the request had been granted.

'As you have done to others,' replied Monedowa, 'so shall it be done to you.'

And seizing the wicked manito, he dashed him against the pillar of stone. His kindred, who were looking on in horror, raised a cry of fear and fled away in a body to some distant land, whence they have never returned.

The widow's family left the scene, and when they had all come out into the open fields, they walked on together until they had reached the fragrant bank and the evergreen wood, where the daughter had first encountered her bird lover.

Monedowa turning to her, said: 'My mother, here we must part. Your daughter and myself must now leave you. The Good Spirit, moved with pity, has allowed me to be your friend. I have done that for which I was sent. I am permitted to take with me the one whom I love. I have found your daughter ever kind, gentle and just. She shall be my companion. The blessing of the Good Spirit be ever with you. Farewell, my mother – my brother, farewell.'

While the widow woman was still lost in wonder at these words, Monedowa and Minda, his wife, changed at the same moment, rose into the air, as beautiful birds, clothed in shining colours of red and blue.

They carolled together as they flew, and their songs were happy, and falling, falling, like clear drops, as they rose, and rose, and winged their way far upward, a delicious peace came into the mind of the poor widow woman, and she returned to her lodge deeply thankful at heart for all the goodness that had been shown to her by the Master of Life.

From that day forth, she never knew want, and her young son proved a comfort to her lodge, and the tuneful carol of Monedowa and Minda, as it fell from heaven, was a music always, go whither she would, sounding peace and joy in her ear.

From: The Indian Fairy Book

The Tortoise with a Pretty Daughter

THERE WAS ONCE a king who was very powerful.

He had great influence over the wild beasts and animals. Now the tortoise was looked upon as the wisest of all beasts and men. This king had a son named Ekpenyon, to whom he gave fifty young girls as wives, but the prince did not like any of them.

The king was very angry at this and made a law that if any man had a daughter who was finer than the prince's wives and who found favour in his son's eyes, the girl herself and her father and mother should be killed.

Now about this time, the tortoise and his wife had a daughter who was very beautiful. The mother thought it was not safe to keep such a fine child, as the prince might fall in love with her, so she told her husband that her daughter ought to be killed and thrown away into the bush.

The tortoise, however, was unwilling, and hid her until she was three years old. One day, when both the tortoise and his wife were away on their farm, the king's son happened to be hunting near their house, and saw a bird perched on the top of the fence round the house.

The bird was watching the little girl and was so entranced with her beauty that he did not notice the prince coming. The prince shot the bird with his bow and arrow, and it dropped inside the fence, so the prince sent his servant to gather it.

While the servant was looking for the bird, he came across the little girl, and was so struck with her form, that he immediately returned to his master and told him what he had seen. The prince then broke down the fence and found the child and fell in love with her at once. He stayed and talked with her for a long time, until at last she agreed to become his wife. He then went home but concealed from his father the fact that he had fallen in love with the beautiful daughter of the tortoise.

But the next morning he sent for the treasurer and got sixty pieces of cloth and three hundred rods and sent them to the tortoise. Then in the early afternoon he went down to the tortoise's house and told him that he wished to marry his daughter.

The tortoise saw at once that what he had dreaded had come to pass, and that his life was in danger, so he told the prince that if the king knew, he would kill not only himself (the tortoise), but also his wife and daughter. The prince replied that he would be killed himself before he allowed the tortoise and his wife and daughter to be killed. Eventually, after much argument, the tortoise consented, and agreed to hand his daughter to the prince as his wife when she arrived at the proper age.

Then the prince went home and told his mother what he had done. She was in great distress at the thought that she would lose her son, of whom she was very proud, as she knew that when the king heard of his son's disobedience, he would kill him.

However, the queen, although she knew how angry her husband would be, wanted her son to marry the girl he had fallen in love with, so she went to the tortoise and gave him some money, clothes, yams, and palm-oil as further dowry on her son's behalf in order that the tortoise should not give his daughter to another man.

For the next five years, the prince was constantly with the tortoise's daughter, whose name was Adet, and when she was about to be put in the fatting house, the prince told his father that he was going to take Adet as his wife. On hearing this the king was very angry and sent word all round his kingdom that all people should come on a certain day to the marketplace to hear the palaver. When the appointed day arrived, the marketplace was quite full of people, and the stones belonging to the king and queen were placed in the middle of the marketplace.

When the king and queen arrived all the people stood up and greeted them, and they then sat down on their stones. The king then told his attendants to bring the girl Adet before him. Upon her arrival, the king was quite astonished at her beauty. He then told the people that he had sent for them to tell them that he was angry with his son for disobeying him and taking Adet as his wife without his knowledge, but that now he had seen her himself he had to acknowledge that she was very beautiful, and that his son had made a good choice. He would therefore forgive his son.

When the people saw the girl, they agreed that she was very fine and quite worthy of being the prince's wife, and begged the king to cancel the law he had made altogether, and the king agreed; and as the law had been made under the 'Egbo' law, he sent for eight Egbos, and told them that the order was cancelled throughout his kingdom, and that for the future no one would be killed who had a daughter more beautiful than the prince's wives, and gave the Egbos palm wine and money to remove the law, and sent them away. Then he declared that the tortoise's daughter, Adet, should marry his son, and he made them marry the same day.

A great feast was then given which lasted for fifty days, and the king killed five cows and gave all the people plenty of foo-foo and palm-oil chop and placed a large number of pots of palm wine in the streets for the people to drink as they liked.

The women brought a big play to the king's compound, and there was singing and dancing kept up day and night during the whole time. The prince and his companions also played in the market square.

When the feast was over, the king gave half of his kingdom to the tortoise to rule over, and three hundred slaves to work on his farm. The prince also gave his father-in-law two hundred women and one hundred girls to work for him, so the tortoise became one of the richest men in the kingdom.

The prince and his wife lived together for a good many years until the king died, when the prince ruled in his place. And all this shows that the tortoise is the wisest of all men and animals.

THE TORTOISE WITH A PRETTY DAUGHTER

Moral: Always have pretty daughters, as no matter how poor they may be, there is always the chance that the king's son may fall in love with them, and they may thus become members of the royal house and obtain much wealth.

From: Folk-Stories from Southern Nigeria

The Jelly Fish Takes a Journey

ONCE UPON A time the jellyfish was a very handsome fellow.

His form was beautiful, and round as the full moon. He had glittering scales and fins and a tail as other fishes have, but he had more than these. He had little feet as well, so that he could walk upon the land as well as swim in the sea. He was merry and he was gay, he was beloved and trusted of the Dragon King.

In spite of all this, his grandmother always said he would come to a bad end, because he would not mind his books at school. She was right. It all came about in this wise.

The Dragon King was but lately wed, when the young Lady Dragon his wife fell very sick. She took to her bed and stayed there, and wise folk in Dragonland shook their heads and said her last day was at hand. Doctors came from far and near, and they dosed her, and they bled her, but no good at all could they do her, the poor young thing, nor recover her of her sickness.

The Dragon King was beside himself. 'Heart's Desire,' he said to his pale bride, 'I would give my life for you.'

'Little good would it do me,' she answered. 'Howbeit, if you will fetch me a monkey's liver, I will eat it and live.'

'A monkey's liver!' cried the Dragon King. 'A monkey's liver! You talk wildly, O light of mine eyes. How shall I find a monkey's liver? Know you not, sweet one, that monkeys dwell in the trees of the forest, whilst we are in the deep sea?'

Tears ran down the Dragon Queen's lovely countenance. 'If I do not have the monkey's liver, I shall die,' she said.

Then the Dragon went forth and called to him the jellyfish. 'The Queen must have a monkey's liver,' he said, 'to cure her of her sickness.'

'What will she do with the monkey's liver?' asked the jellyfish.

'Why, she will eat it,' said the Dragon King.

'Oh!' said the jellyfish.

'Now,' said the king, 'you must go and fetch me a live monkey. I have heard that they dwell in the tall trees of the forest. Therefore, swim quickly, O jellyfish, and bring a monkey with you back again.'

'How will I get the monkey to come back with me?' said the jellyfish.

'Tell him of all the beauties and pleasures of Dragonland. Tell him he will be happy here and that he may play with mermaids all the day long.'

'Well,' said the jellyfish, 'I'll tell him that.'

Off set the jellyfish; and he swam, and he swam, till at last he reached the shore where grew the tall trees of the forest. And, sure enough, there was a monkey sitting in the branches of a persimmon tree, eating persimmons.

'The very thing,' said the jellyfish to himself; 'I'm in luck.

'Noble monkey,' he said, 'will you come to Dragonland with me?'

'How should I get there?' said the monkey.

'Only sit on my back,' said the jellyfish, 'and I'll take you there; you'll have no trouble at all.'

'Why should I go there, after all?' said the monkey. 'I am very well off as I am.'

'Ah,' said the jellyfish, 'it's plain that you know little of all the beauties and pleasures of Dragonland. There you will be happy as the day is long. You will win great riches and honour. Besides, you may play with the mermaids from morn till eve.'

'I'll come,' said the monkey.

And he slipped down from the persimmon tree and jumped on the jelly-fish's back.

When the two of them were about halfway over to Dragonland, the jellyfish laughed.

'Now, jellyfish, why do you laugh?'

'I laugh for joy,' said the jellyfish. 'When you come to Dragonland, my master, the Dragon King, will get your liver, and give it to my mistress the Dragon Queen to eat, and then she will recover from her sickness.'

'My liver?' said the monkey.

'Why, of course,' said the jellyfish.

'Alas and alack,' cried the monkey, 'I'm grieved indeed, but if it's my liver you're wanting I haven't it with me. To tell you the truth, it weighs pretty heavy, so I just took it out and hung it upon a branch of that persimmon tree where you found me. Quick, quick, let's go back for it.'

Back they went, and the monkey was up in the persimmon tree in a twinkling.

'Mercy me, I don't see it at all,' he said. 'Where can I have mislaid it? I should not be surprised if some rascal has stolen it,' he said.

Now if the jellyfish had minded his books at school, would he have been hoodwinked by the monkey? You may believe not. But his grandmother always said he would come to a bad end.

'I shall be some time finding it,' said the monkey. 'You'd best be getting home to Dragonland. The prince would be loath for you to be out after dark. You can call for me another day. *Sayonara.*'

The monkey and the jellyfish parted on the best of terms.

The minute the Dragon King set eyes on the jellyfish, 'Where's the monkey?' he said.

'I'm to call for him another day,' said the jellyfish. And he told all the tale.

The Dragon King flew into a towering rage. He called his executioners and bid them beat the jellyfish.

'Break every bone in his body,' he cried; 'beat him to a jelly.'

Alas for the sad fate of the jellyfish! Jelly he remains to this very day.

As for the young Dragon Queen, she was fain to laugh when she heard the story.

'If I can't have a monkey's liver, I must needs do without it,' she said. 'Give me my best brocade gown and I will get up, for I feel a good deal better.'

From: Green Willow & Other Japanese Fairy Tales

Jack the Giant-killer

WHEN GOOD KING Arthur reigned, there lived near the Land's End of England, in the county of Cornwall, a farmer who had one only son called Jack. He was brisk and of a ready lively wit, so that nobody or nothing could worst him.

In those days the Mount of Cornwall was kept by a huge giant named 'Cormoran'. He was eighteen feet in height, and about three yards round the waist, of a fierce and grim countenance, the terror of all the neighbouring towns and villages. He lived in a cave in the midst of the Mount, and whenever he wanted food, he would wade over to the mainland, where he would furnish himself with whatever came in his way.

Everybody at his approach ran out of their houses, while he seized on their cattle, making nothing of carrying half-a-dozen oxen on his back at a time; and as for their sheep and hogs, he would tie them round his waist like a bunch of tallow-dips. He had done this for many years, so that all Cornwall was in despair.

One day Jack happened to be at the town hall when the magistrates were sitting in council about the Giant. He asked: 'What reward will be given to the man who kills Cormoran?'

'The giant's treasure,' they said, 'will be the reward.'

Quoth Jack: 'Then let me undertake it.'

So, he got a horn, shovel, and pickaxe, and went over to the Mount in the beginning of a dark winter's evening, when he fell to work, and before morning had dug a pit twenty-two feet deep, and nearly as broad, covering it over with long sticks and straw. Then he strewed a little mould over it, so that it appeared like plain ground.

Jack then placed himself on the opposite side of the pit, farthest from the giant's lodging, and, just at the break of day, he put the horn to his mouth, and blew, Tantivy, Tantivy.

This noise roused the giant, who rushed from his cave, crying: 'You incorrigible villain, are you come here to disturb my rest? You shall pay dearly for this. Satisfaction I will have, and this it shall be, I will take you whole and broil you for breakfast.'

He had no sooner uttered this, than he tumbled into the pit, and made the very foundations of the Mount to shake.

'Oh, Giant,' quoth Jack, 'where are you now? Oh, faith, you are gotten now into Lob's Pound, where I will surely plague you for your threatening words: what do you think now of broiling me for your breakfast? Will no other diet serve you but poor Jack?'

Then having tantalised the giant for a while, he gave him a most weighty knock with his pickaxe on the very crown of his head and killed him on the spot.

Jack then filled up the pit with earth, and went to search the cave, which he found contained much treasure. When the magistrates heard of this, they made a declaration he should henceforth be termed, 'Jack the Giant-killer', and presented him with a sword and a belt, on which were written these words embroidered in letters of gold: 'Here's the right valiant Cornish man, who slew the giant Cormoran'.

The news of Jack's victory soon spread over all the West of England, so that another giant, named Blunderbore, hearing of it, vowed to be revenged on Jack, if ever he should light on him. This giant was the lord of an enchanted castle situated in the midst of a lonesome wood.

Now Jack, about four months afterwards, walking near this wood in his journey to Wales, being weary, seated himself near a pleasant fountain and fell fast asleep.

While he was sleeping, the giant, coming there for water, discovered him, and knew him to be the far-famed Jack the Giant-killer by the lines written on the belt. Without ado, he took Jack on his shoulders and carried him towards his castle.

Now, as they passed through a thicket, the rustling of the boughs awakened Jack, who was strangely surprised to find himself in the clutches of the giant. His terror was only begun for, on entering the castle, he saw the ground strewed with human bones, and the giant told him his own would ere long be among them.

After this the giant locked poor Jack in an immense chamber, leaving him there while he went to fetch another giant, his brother, living in the same wood, who might share in the meal on Jack.

After waiting some time Jack, upon going to the window, beheld afar off the two giants coming towards the castle.

'Now,' quoth Jack to himself, 'my death or my deliverance is at hand.'

Now, there were strong cords in a corner of the room in which Jack was, and two of these he took, and made a strong noose at the end; and while the giants were unlocking the iron gate of the castle, he threw the ropes over each of their heads.

Then he drew the other ends across a beam, and pulled with all his might, so that he throttled them. Then, when he saw they were black in the face, he slid down the rope, and drawing his sword, slew them both. Then, taking the giant's keys and unlocking the rooms, he found three fair ladies tied by the hair of their heads, almost starved to death.

'Sweet ladies,' quoth Jack, 'I have destroyed this monster and his brutish brother and obtained your liberties.'

This said he presented them with the keys, and so proceeded on his journey to Wales.

Jack made the best of his way by travelling as fast as he could, but lost his road, and was benighted, and could find any habitation until, coming into a narrow valley, he found a large house, and in order to get shelter took courage to knock at the gate.

But what was his surprise when there came forth a monstrous giant with two heads; yet he did not appear so fiery as the others were, for he was a Welsh giant, and what he did was by private and secret malice under the false show of friendship. Jack, having told his condition to the giant, was shown into a bedroom, where, in the dead of night, he heard his host in another apartment muttering these words:

'Though here you lodge with me this night,
You shall not see the morning light
My club shall dash your brains outright!'

'Say you so,' quoth Jack; 'that is like one of your Welsh tricks, yet I hope to be cunning enough for you.'

Then, getting out of bed, he laid a billet in the bed in his stead, and hid himself in a corner of the room. At the dead time of the night in came the Welsh giant, who struck several heavy blows on the bed with his club, thinking he had broken every bone in Jack's skin. The next morning Jack, laughing in his sleeve, gave him hearty thanks for his night's lodging.

'How have you rested?' quoth the giant; 'did you not feel anything in the night?'

'No,' quoth Jack, 'nothing but a rat, which gave me two or three slaps with her tail.'

With that, greatly wondering, the giant led Jack to breakfast, bringing him a bowl containing four gallons of hasty pudding.

Being loth to let the giant think it too much for him, Jack put a large leather bag under his loose coat, in such a way that he could convey the pudding into it without its being perceived. Then, telling the giant he would show him a trick, taking a knife, Jack ripped open the bag, and out came all the hasty pudding.

Whereupon, saying, 'Odds splutters hur nails, hur can do that trick hurself,' the monster took the knife, and ripping open his belly, fell down dead.

Now, it happened in these days that King Arthur's only son asked his father to give him a large sum of money in order that he might go and seek his fortune in the principality of Wales, where lived a beautiful lady possessed with seven evil spirits. The king did his best to persuade his son from it, but in vain; so, at last gave way and the prince set out with two horses, one loaded with money, the other for himself to ride upon.

Now, after several days' travel, he came to a market town in Wales, where he beheld a vast crowd of people gathered together. The prince asked the reason of it and was told that they had arrested a corpse for several large sums of money which the deceased owed when he died.

The prince replied that it was a pity creditors should be so cruel, and said: 'Go bury the dead, and let his creditors come to my lodging, and there their debts shall be paid.'

They came, in such great numbers that before night he had only twopence left for himself.

Now Jack the Giant-killer, coming that way, was so taken with the generosity of the prince, that he desired to be his servant. This being agreed upon, the next morning they set forward on their journey together, when, as they were riding out of the town, an old woman called after the prince, saying, 'He has owed me twopence these seven years; pray pay me as well as the rest.'

Putting his hand to his pocket, the prince gave the woman all he had left, so that after their day's food, which cost what small spell Jack had by him, they were without a penny between them.

When the sun got low, the king's son said: 'Jack, since we have no money, where can we lodge this night?'

But Jack replied: 'Master, we'll do well enough, for I have an uncle lives within two miles of this place; he is a huge and monstrous giant with three heads; he'll fight five hundred men in armour, and make them to fly before him.'

'Alas!' quoth the prince, 'what shall we do there? He'll certainly chop us up at a mouthful. Nay, we are scarce enough to fill one of his hollow teeth!'

'It is no matter for that,' quoth Jack; 'I myself will go before and prepare the way for you; therefore, stop here and wait till I return.'

Jack then rode away at full speed, and coming to the gate of the castle, he knocked so loud that he made the neighbouring hills resound.

The giant roared out at this like thunder: 'Who's there?'

Jack answered: 'None but your poor cousin Jack.'

Quoth he: 'What news with my poor cousin Jack?'

He replied: 'Dear uncle, heavy news, God wot!'

'Prithee,' quoth the giant, 'what heavy news can come to me? I am a giant with three heads, and besides you know I can fight five hundred men in armour, and make them fly like chaff before the wind.'

'Oh, but,' quoth Jack, 'here's the king's son a-coming with a thousand men in armour to kill you and destroy all that you have!'

'Oh, cousin Jack,' said the giant, 'this is heavy news indeed! I will immediately run and hide myself, and you shall lock, bolt, and bar me in, and keep the keys until the prince is gone.'

Having secured the giant, Jack fetched his master, when they made themselves heartily merry whilst the poor giant lay trembling in a vault under the ground.

Early in the morning, Jack furnished his master with a fresh supply of gold and silver, and then sent him three miles forward on his journey, at which time the prince was pretty well out of the smell of the giant. Jack then returned, and let the giant out of the vault, who asked what he should give him for keeping the castle from destruction.

'Why,' quoth Jack, 'I want nothing but the old coat and cap, together with the old rusty sword and slippers which are at your bed's head.'

Quoth the giant: 'You know not what you ask; they are the most precious things I have. The coat will keep you invisible, the cap will tell you all you want to know, the sword cuts asunder whatever you strike, and the shoes are of extraordinary swiftness. But you have been very serviceable to me, therefore take them with all my heart.'

Jack thanked his uncle, and then went off with them. He soon overtook his master and they quickly arrived at the house of the lady the prince sought, who, finding the prince to be a suitor, prepared a splendid banquet for him.

After the repast was concluded, she told him she had a task for him. She wiped his mouth with a handkerchief, saying: 'You must show me that handkerchief tomorrow morning, or else you will lose your head.'

With that she put it in her bosom. The prince went to bed in great sorrow, but Jack's cap of knowledge informed him how it was to be obtained. In the middle of the night, she called upon her familiar spirit to carry her to Lucifer.

But Jack put on his coat of darkness and his shoes of swiftness and was there as soon as she was. When she entered the place of the Old One, she gave the handkerchief to old Lucifer, who laid it upon a shelf, whence Jack took it and brought it to his master, who showed it to the lady next day, and so saved his life. On that day, she gave the prince a kiss and told him he must show her the lips tomorrow morning that she kissed last night or lose his head.

'Ah!' he replied, 'if you kiss none but mine, I will.'

'That is neither here nor there,' said she; 'if you do not, death's your portion!'

At midnight she went as before and was angry with old Lucifer for letting the handkerchief go.

'But now,' quoth she, 'I will be too hard for the king's son, for I will kiss thee, and he is to show me thy lips.'

Which she did, and Jack, when she was not standing by, cut off Lucifer's head and brought it under his invisible coat to his master, who the next morning pulled it out by the horns before the lady. This broke the enchantment and the evil spirit left her, and she appeared in all her beauty. They were married the next morning, and soon after went to the court of King Arthur, where Jack for his many great exploits, was made one of the Knights of the Round Table.

Jack soon went searching for giants again, but he had not ridden far, when he saw a cave, near the entrance of which he beheld a giant sitting upon a block of timber, with a knotted iron club by his side. His goggle eyes were like flames of fire, his countenance grim and ugly, and his cheeks like a couple of large flitches of bacon, while the bristles of his beard resembled rods of iron wire, and the locks that hung down upon his brawny shoulders were like curled snakes or hissing adders.

Jack alighted from his horse, and, putting on the coat of darkness, went up close to the giant, and said softly: 'Oh! are you there? It will not be long before I take you fast by the beard.'

The giant all this while could not see him, on account of his invisible coat, so that Jack, coming up close to the monster, struck a blow with his sword at his head, but, missing his aim, he cut off the nose instead.

At this, the giant roared like claps of thunder, and began to lay about him with his iron club like one stark mad. But Jack, running behind, drove his sword up to the hilt in the giant's back, so that he fell down dead. This done, Jack cut off the giant's head and sent it, with his brother's also, to King Arthur, by a waggoner he hired for that purpose.

Jack now resolved to enter the giant's cave in search of his treasure and, passing along through a great many windings and turnings, he came at length to a large room paved with freestone, at the upper end of which was a boiling caldron, and on the right hand a large table, at which the giant used to dine. Then he came to a window, barred with iron, through which he looked and beheld a vast number of miserable captives, who, seeing him, cried out: 'Alas! Young man, are you come to be one amongst us in this miserable den?'

'Ay,' quoth Jack, 'but pray tell me what is the meaning of your captivity?'

'We are kept here,' said one, 'till such time as the giants have a wish to feast, and then the fattest among us is slaughtered! And many are the times they have dined upon murdered men!'

'Say you so,' quoth Jack, and straightway unlocked the gate and let them free, who all rejoiced like condemned men at sight of a pardon.

Then searching the giant's coffers, he shared the gold and silver equally amongst them and took them to a neighbouring castle, where they all feasted and made merry over their deliverance.

But in the midst of all this mirth, a messenger brought news that one Thunderdell, a giant with two heads, having heard of the death of his kinsmen, had come from the northern dales to be revenged on Jack, and was within a mile of the castle, the country people flying before him like chaff.

But Jack was not a bit daunted, and said: 'Let him come! I have a tool to pick his teeth; and you, ladies and gentlemen, walk out into the garden, and you shall witness this giant Thunderdell's death and destruction.'

The castle was situated in the midst of a small island surrounded by a moat thirty feet deep and twenty feet wide, over which lay a drawbridge. So, Jack employed men to cut through this bridge on both sides, nearly to the middle; and then, dressing himself in his invisible coat, he marched against the giant with his sword of sharpness. Although the giant could not see Jack, he smelt his approach, and cried out in these words:

'Fee, fi, fo, fum!
I smell the blood of an Englishman!
Be he alive or be he dead,
I'll grind his bones to make me bread!'

'Say you so,' said Jack; 'then you are a monstrous miller indeed.'

The giant cried out again: 'Are you that villain who killed my kinsmen? Then I will tear you with my teeth, suck your blood, and grind your bones to powder.'

'You'll have to catch me first,' quoth Jack, and throwing off his invisible coat, so that the giant might see him, and putting on his shoes of swiftness, he ran from the giant, who followed like a walking castle, so that the very foundations of the earth seemed to shake at every step.

Jack led him a long dance, in order that the gentlemen and ladies might see; and at last, to end the matter, ran lightly over the drawbridge, the giant, in full speed, pursuing him with his club.

Then, coming to the middle of the bridge, the giant's great weight broke it down, and he tumbled headlong into the water, where he rolled and wallowed like a whale. Jack, standing by the moat, laughed at him all the while; but though the giant foamed to hear him scoff, and plunged from place to place in the moat, yet he could not get out to be revenged. Jack at length got a cart-rope and cast it over the two heads of the giant, and drew him ashore by a team of horses, and then cut off both his heads with his sword of sharpness and sent them to King Arthur.

After some time spent in mirth and pastime, Jack, taking leave of the knights and ladies, set out for new adventures. Through many woods he passed and came at length to the foot of a high mountain. Here, late at night, he found a lonesome house, and knocked at the door, which was opened by an aged man with a head as white as snow.

'Father,' said Jack, 'can you lodge a benighted traveller that has lost his way?'

'Yes,' said the old man; 'you are right welcome to my poor cottage.'

Whereupon Jack entered, and down they sat together, and the old man began to speak as follows: 'Son, I see by your belt you are the great conqueror of giants, and behold, my son, on the top of this mountain is an enchanted castle, this is kept by a giant named Galligantua, and he by the help of an old conjurer, betrays many knights and ladies into his castle, where by magic art they are transformed into sundry shapes and forms.

'But above all, I grieve for a duke's daughter, whom they fetched from her father's garden, carrying her through the air in a burning chariot drawn by fiery dragons, when they secured her within the castle, and transformed her into a white hind.

'And though many knights have tried to break the enchantment, and work her deliverance, yet no one could accomplish it, on account of two dreadful griffins which are placed at the castle gate, and which destroy everyone who comes near. But you, my son, may pass by them undiscovered, where on the gates of the castle you will find engraved in large letters how the spell may be broken.'

Jack gave the old man his hand and promised that in the morning he would venture his life to free the lady.

In the morning Jack arose and put on his invisible coat and magic cap and shoes and prepared himself for the fray. Now, when he had reached the top of the mountain, he soon discovered the two fiery griffins, but passed them without fear, because of his invisible coat.

When he had got beyond them, he found upon the gates of the castle a golden trumpet hung by a silver chain, under which these lines were engraved:

'Whoever shall this trumpet blow,
Shall soon the giant overthrow,
And break the black enchantment straight;
So all shall be in happy state.'

Jack had no sooner read this, but he blew the trumpet, at which the castle trembled to its vast foundations, and the giant and conjurer were in horrid confusion, biting their thumbs and tearing their hair, knowing their wicked reign was at an end. Then the giant stooping to take up his club, Jack at one blow cut off his head; whereupon the conjurer, mounting up into the air, was carried away in a whirlwind.

Then the enchantment was broken, and all the lords and ladies who had so long been transformed into birds and beasts returned to their proper shapes, and the castle vanished away in a cloud of smoke.

This being done, the head of Galligantua was likewise, in the usual manner, conveyed to the Court of King Arthur, where, the very next day, Jack followed, with the knights and ladies who had been delivered.

Whereupon, as a reward for his good services, the king prevailed upon the duke to bestow his daughter in marriage on honest Jack.

So married they were, and the whole kingdom was filled with joy at the wedding. Furthermore, the king bestowed on Jack a noble castle, with a very beautiful estate thereto belonging, where he and his lady lived in great joy and happiness all the rest of their days.

From: English Fairy Tales

The Enchanted Mule

THERE WAS ONCE a very merry, but very poor hostler in Salamanca. He was so poor that he had to go about his business in rags; and one day when he was attending on the richly caparisoned mule belonging to the Archbishop of Toledo, he gave vent to his feelings in words.

'Ah,' said he, 'my father was always called a donkey from the day of his marriage; but would to goodness I were the archbishop's mule! Look at the rich livery he bears; look at his stout sides; see how he drinks up his wine and eats his maize bread! Oh, it would be a merry life, indeed! My father was, they say, an ass, so I would be a mule!'

And then he leant against the manger and laughed so heartily that the archbishop's mule stopped eating to look at him.

'What ho!' said the mule. 'Remember that my reverend master, being a corpulent man, is somewhat heavy; but if you will change conditions with me, you need but take hold of both my ears, and, *caramba*, a mule you shall be, and that in the service of the Archbishop of Toledo!'

'And that will I,' answered Pablo the hostler; 'for better be a well-fed mule than a starving hostler.'

So saying, he seized the mule by the ears, and, looking at him in the face, he was immediately transformed; but, to his surprise, he saw that the quondam mule was changed into a monk.

'How now!' cried he. 'Wilt thou not bring me some more wine and maize bread, sir monk? Wilt thou not be my hostler?'

But the monk turned away and left the stable, and Pablo then saw that he had made a mistake. But he resolved that as soon as he was led out into the street he would run off to his old mother and implore her to intercede on his behalf with the patron St. James of Compostella.

When the archbishop had rested, he called for his mule, which was brought out; and, in the absence of the hostler, whom they could not find, one of the attendants was about tightening the girths, when the mule Pablo, seizing the opportunity, bolted away as hard as he could down the road in the direction of his mother's house.

The archbishop thought his mule had gone mad, and as the servants followed it, running, and crying out, 'Stop the beast – stop it!' the rabble joined in the chase; but Pablo never stopped till he got to his mother's house.

The old woman was at the door, spinning at her distaff, and as she was very deaf, she had not heard the clamour. Pablo, bending over her, tried to kiss her hand to ask her for her blessing, but his tongue now failed him. So frightened was she at the approach of the animal that she hit him over the head with her distaff, and cried out, 'Abernuncio!'

By this time the servants had surrounded him, and were trying to lead him back, but he would not go. He stood on his hind-legs, and then lay down on his side, and rolled in the dust till the scarlet saddlecloth was spoilt, and then, suddenly rising, rushed into the cottage, and tried to sit on his accustomed chair.

His mother fled the house, and the rabble entered, and so cudgelled Pablo that he was fain to return to the inn; and, after being groomed, he allowed the archbishop to mount him. However, he had not gone far before he exclaimed, 'By St. Iago, this mule hath the pace of a camel!'

Pablo, not being accustomed to four legs, did not know how to use them, so that he would move his right fore and hind legs together. This caused the archbishop great inconvenience, for, being a corpulent man, it made him roll about on the saddle like the gold ball on the cathedral of Sevilla, when the west wind loosened it, and the east wind blew it down.

Seizing the pommel with both his hands, and raising himself in his shoe stirrups, he looked as if he intended to vault over the head of the mule; and as they were at this moment going through a village, the inhabitants, who had come out to see the archbishop, thought he was about to deliver a sermon. So, surrounding the mule, they uncovered their heads, and knelt awaiting the blessing.

Pablo, forgetting he was a mule, thought the people were doing homage to him, and being of a merry disposition, he gave way to such inward laughter that it brought on a violent fit of coughing, which the faithful – not seeing the face of the archbishop, for they devoutly bent their heads towards the ground – took to be the natural clearing of the throat before speaking.

But the archbishop, who was now becoming seriously frightened, and thinking that the evil one had entered the body of his mule, exclaimed, '*Exorciso te – abernuncio!*'

Then did Pablo sit down on his hindquarters, so that the archbishop slid off the saddle and rolled on the ground, and another '*Abernuncio!*' in a deeper tone, brought the devout people to their feet. Pablo at this moment got up, and by so doing completely capsized the venerable archbishop, causing him to turn over on to his head. Full of dust and anger, the prelate started to his feet, and carefully examined his mule to see if he could account for this peculiar behaviour.

Sorely grieved did Pablo feel at having caused the good archbishop so much annoyance, and, so as to show his contrition, he went down on his forelegs, thinking to kneel, which so frightened all the people that they instinctively took shelter behind the archbishop. But he was as much afraid as the rest, and had it not been that they held him by his robes, he would have run away.

'This beats the mule of Merida,' cried one, 'who ran away with the miller's wife and then regretted the bargain. See, he is craving for pardon.'

Pablo the mule rose after kneeling for some time, and, after the fashion of trained animals of this breed, he extended his fore and hindlegs, so as to facilitate the archbishop mounting him, which he soon did, feeling convinced that the mule had intended no harm; but Pablo, regretting his mistake and the loss of time it had caused, set off at a quick amble, which so disconcerted his rider that he had to hold on by the pommel and the crupper; and thus he was hurried out of the village, and the people were done out of the blessing.

The attendants, who were on foot, tried to keep up with Pablo; but this they could not do, owing to his long strides; and not until they were within sight of Toledo did they get up to their master, who, by this time, was out of breath and countenance.

They, fearing that the mule might start off again, placed a man on each side holding the reins, and thus did they approach the eastern gate of the city, at which many priests were waiting with the cross and the sword of the archbishop, in order to give him a fitting welcome, according to the rules of the Church.

Pablo, seeing the large silver cross, the emblem of Christianity, slackened his pace, and when within a few yards of it, in obedience to what his mother had taught him as a child, dropped down on his knees, bending his head to the ground; but this he did so suddenly, that the archbishop fell off the saddle on to his neck, and, to break his fall, caught hold of his servants by their ears, nearly tearing them off, and causing them also to tumble.

Thinking that the evil one had seized them, they struck out right and left, and nearly stunned their master with the blows and kicks. Pablo, hoping to retrieve his fortune, started to his legs with the archbishop clinging round his neck, and galloped after the two servants with his mouth open, so that, should he catch them, he might bite them. But they, surmising what he meant, sought refuge among the priests, and these in their turn made haste to get into a small chapel close by.

'Our archbishop must have changed mules with Beelzebub,' said a fat priest, 'for no earthly animal would thus treat a prince of the Church!'

'Ay,' continued one of the runaway servants; 'and if his neck had been a foot longer, I should have been dangling in mid-air like the coffin of the false prophet.'

'I never thought to have run so fast again,' ejaculated a very short and stout priest.

'Faith, my legs seemed to grow under me, as our sacristan said after he had been tossed by the abbot's bull.'

'But what has become of the archbishop?' said another. 'We must not leave him in his sorry plight.'

Saying this, he carefully opened the door of the chapel, and there they saw their prelate swooning on the pavement, and Pablo dashing full tilt among the crowd, trying to wreak his vengeance on as many as he could possibly get hold of.

Having torn the leather breeches of some half-dozen sightseers and knocked down and trampled on some score of men and women, he rushed out of the city by the same gate, and never stopped till he arrived at the inn where he had been hostler. The master of the inn, thinking that some mishap had befallen the archbishop, made haste to secure the mule; but as it was already night, he postponed sending off one of his servants till next morning.

Once again at the manger, Pablo had time to consider over the mistake he had made, and he would gladly have undergone any punishment, could he but have regained his former shape.

While he was thus musing, he saw the monk approaching, looking very sorrowful indeed.

'Pablo,' said he, 'how dost thou like being a mule?'

Now, Pablo was cunning, and, not wishing to let the monk know what had happened, he answered, 'As for liking it, I enjoyed carrying the archbishop as much as he liked being carried; but I am not accustomed to such gay trappings and good living, so that I am afraid of injuring my health.'

'If that be the case,' continued the monk, 'hold down thy head, and I will relieve thee of the danger; for, to tell you the truth, I find out that my wife is still living, and she recognized me although I was disguised as a monk. By my faith, I would rather bear my master's harness to the grave than my wife's tongue from morning till night! *Caramba*, I hear her knocking at the door! Dear Pablo, let us again exchange conditions.'

And Pablo, when he awoke next morning, was tightly grasping a beam, thinking he was the Archbishop of Toledo clinging on to the mule's neck.

From: Tales from The Lands of Nuts & Grapes

The Fisherman's Son & the Gruagach of Tricks

THERE WAS AN old fisherman once in Erin who had a wife and one son.

The old fisherman used to go about with a fishing-rod and tackle to the rivers and lochs and every place where fish resort, and he was killing salmon and other fish to keep the life in himself and his wife and son.

The son was not so keen nor so wise as another, and the father was instructing him every day in fishing, so that if himself should be taken from the world, the son would be able to support the old mother and get his own living.

One day, when the father and son were fishing in a river near the sea, they looked out over the water and saw a small dark speck on the waves. It grew larger and larger, till they saw a boat, and when the boat drew near, they saw a man sitting in the stern of it.

There was a nice beach near the place where they were fishing. The man brought the boat straight to the beach, and stepping out drew it up on the sand.

They saw then that the stranger was a man of high degree (*duine uasal*).

After he had put the boat high on the sand, he came to where the two were at work, and said: 'Old fisherman, you'd better let this son of yours with me for a year and a day, and I will make a very wise man of him. I am the Gruagach na g-cleasan (Gruagach of tricks), and I'll bind myself to be here with your son this day year.'

'I can't let him go,' said the old fisherman, 'till he gets his mother's advice.'

'Whatever goes as far as women I'll have nothing to do with,' said the Gruagach. 'You had better give him to me now, and let the mother alone.'

They talked till at last the fisherman promised to let his son go for the year and a day. Then the Gruagach gave his word to have the boy there at the seashore that day year.

The Gruagach and the boy went into the boat and sailed away.

When the year and a day were over, the old fisherman went to the same place where he had parted with his son and the Gruagach, and stood looking over the sea, thinking would he see his son that day.

At last, he saw a black spot on the water, then a boat.

When it was near, he saw two men sitting in the stern of the boat. When it touched land, the two, who were *duine uasal* in appearance, jumped out, and one of them pulled the boat to the top of the strand. Then that one, followed by the other, came to where the old fisherman was waiting, and asked: 'What trouble is on you now, my good man?'

'I had a son that wasn't so keen nor so wise as another, and myself and this son were here fishing, and a stranger came, like yourself today, and asked would I let my son with him for a year and a day. I let the son go, and the man promised to be here with him today, and that's why I am waiting at this place now.'

'Well,' said the Gruagach, 'am I your son?'

'You are not,' said the fisherman.

'Is this man here your son?'

'I don't know him,' said the fisherman.

'Well, then, he is all you will have in place of your son,' said the Gruagach.

The old man looked again and knew his son. He caught hold of him and welcomed him home.

'Now,' said the Gruagach, 'isn't he a better man than he was a year ago?'

'Oh, he's nearly a smart man now!' said the old fisherman.

'Well,' said the Gruagach, 'will you let him with me for another year and a day?'

'I will not,' said the old man; 'I want him myself.'

The Gruagach then begged and craved till the fisherman promised to let the son with him for a year and a day again. But the old man forgot to take his word of the Gruagach to bring back the son at the end of the time; and when the Gruagach and the boy were in the boat, and had pushed out to sea, the Gruagach shouted to the old man: 'I kept my promise to bring back your son today. I haven't given you my word at all now. I'll not bring him back, and you'll never see him again.'

The fisherman went home with a heavy and sorrowful heart, and the old woman scolded him all that night till next morning for letting her son go with the Gruagach a second time.

Then himself and the old woman were lamenting a quarter of a year; and when another quarter had passed, he said to her: 'I'll leave you here now, and I'll be walking on myself till I wear my legs off up to my knees, and from my knees to my waist, till I find where is my son.' So away went the old man walking, and he used to spend but one night in a house, and not two nights in any house, till his feet were all in blisters. One evening late, he came to a hut where there was an old woman sitting at a fire.

'Poor man!' said she, when she laid eyes on him, 'it's a great distress you are in, to be so disfigured with wounds and sores. What is the trouble that's on you?'

'I had a son,' said the old man, 'and the Gruagach na g-cleasan came on a day and took him from me.'

'Oh, poor man!' said she. 'I have a son with that same Gruagach these twelve years, and I have never been able to get him back or get sight of him, and I'm in dread you'll not be able to get your son either. But tomorrow, in the morning, I'll tell you all I know, and show you the road you must go to find the house of the Gruagach na g-cleasan.'

Next morning, she showed the old fisherman the road. He was to come to the place by evening.

When he came and entered the house, the Gruagach shook hands with him, and said: 'You are welcome, old fisherman. It was I that put this journey on you, and made you come here looking for your son.'

'It was no one else but you,' said the fisherman.

'Well,' said the Gruagach, 'you won't see your son today. At noon tomorrow, I'll put a whistle in my mouth and call together all the birds in my place, and they'll come. Among

103

others will be twelve doves. I'll put my hand in my pocket, this way, and take out wheat and throw it before them on the ground. The doves will eat the wheat, and you must pick your son out of the twelve. If you find him, you'll have him; if you don't, you'll never get him again.'

After the Gruagach had said these words, the old man ate his supper and went to bed.

In the dead of night, the old fisherman's son came.

'Oh, father!' said he, 'it would be hard for you to pick me out among the twelve doves, if you had to do it alone; but I'll tell you.

'When the Gruagach calls us in, and we go to pick up the wheat, I'll make a ring around the others, walking for myself; and as I go I'll give some of them a tip of my bill, and I'll lift my wings when I'm striking them. There was a spot under one of my arms when I left home, and you'll see that spot under my wing when I raise it tomorrow. Don't miss the bird that I'll be, and don't let your eyes off it; if you do, you'll lose me forever.'

Next morning the old man rose, had his breakfast, and kept thinking of what his son had told him.

At midday the Gruagach took his whistle and blew. Birds came to him from every part, and among others the twelve doves.

He took wheat from his pocket, threw it to the doves, and said to the father: 'Now pick out your son from the twelve.'

The old man was watching, and soon he saw one of the doves walking around the other eleven and hitting some of them a clip of its bill, and then it raised its wings, and the old man saw the spot. The bird let its wings down again and went to eating with the rest.

The father never let his eyes off the bird. After a while he said to the Gruagach: 'I'll have that bird there for my son.'

'Well,' said the Gruagach, 'that is your son. I can't blame you for having him; but I blame your instructor for the information he gave you, and I give him my curse.'

So, the old fisherman got his son back in his proper shape, and away they went, father and son, from the house of the Gruagach. The old man felt stronger now, and they never stopped travelling a day till they came home.

The old mother was very glad to see her son, and see him such a wise, smart man.

After coming home, they had no means but the fishing; they were as poor as ever before.

At this time, it was given out at every crossroad in Erin, and in all public places in the kingdom, that there were to be great horseraces. Now, when the day came, the old fisherman's son said: 'Come away with me, father, to the races.'

The old man went with him, and when they were near the racecourse, the son said: 'Stop here till I tell you this: I'll make myself into the best horse that's here today, and do you take me to the place where the races are to be, and when you take me in, I'll open my mouth, trying to kill and eat every man that'll be near me, I'll have such life and swiftness; and do you find a rider for me that'll ride me, and don't let me go till the other horses are far ahead on the course. Then let me go. I'll come up to them, and I'll run ahead of them and win the race.

After that every rich man there will want to buy me of you; but don't you sell me to any man for less than five hundred pounds; and be sure you get that price for me. And when you have the gold, and you are giving me up, take the bit out of my mouth, and don't sell the bridle for any money. Then come to this spot, shake the bridle, and I'll be here in my own form before you.'

The son made himself a horse, and the old fisherman took him to the race. He reared and snorted, trying to take the head off every man that came near him.

The old man shouted for a rider. A rider came; he mounted the horse and held him in. The old man didn't let him start till the other horses were well ahead on the course; then he let him go.

The new horse caught up with the others and shot past them. So, they had not gone half way when he was in at the winning-post.

When the race was ended, there was a great noise over the strange horse. Men crowded around the old fisherman from every corner of the field, asking what would he take for the horse.

'Five hundred pounds,' said he.

'Here 'tis for you,' said the next man to him.

In a moment the horse was sold, and the money in the old man's pocket. Then he pulled the bridle off the horse's head and made his way out of the place as fast as ever he could.

It was not long till he was at the spot where the son had told him what to do. The minute he came, he shook the bridle, and the son was there before him in his own shape and features.

Oh, but the old fisherman was glad when he had his son with him again, and the money in his pocket!

The two went home together. They had money enough now to live and quit the fishing. They had plenty to eat and drink, and they spent their lives in ease and comfort till the next year, when it was given out at all the crossroads in Erin, and every public place in the kingdom, that there was to be a great hunting with hounds, in the same place where the races had been the year before.

When the day came, the fisherman's son said: 'Come, father, let us go away to this hunting.'

'Ah!' said the old man, 'what do we want to go for? Haven't we plenty to eat at home, with money enough and to spare? What do we care for hunting with hounds?'

'Oh! They'll give us more money,' said the son, 'if we go.'

The fisherman listened to his son, and away they went. When the two came to the spot where the son had made a horse of himself the year before, he stopped, and said to the father: 'I'll make a hound of myself today, and when you bring me in sight of the game, you'll see me wild with jumping and trying to get away; but do you hold me fast till the right time comes, then let go. I'll sweep ahead of every hound in the field, catch the game, and win the prize for you.

'When the hunt is over, so many men will come to buy me that they'll put you in a maze; but be sure you get three hundred pounds for me, and when you have the money, and are giving me up, don't forget to keep my rope. Come to this place, shake the rope, and I'll be here before you, as I am now. If you don't keep the rope, you'll go home without me.'

The son made a hound of himself, and the old father took him to the hunting-ground.

When the hunt began, the hound was springing and jumping like mad; but the father held him till the others were far out in the field. Then he let him loose, and away went the son.

Soon he was up with the pack, then in front of the pack, and never stopped till he caught the game and won the prize.

When the hunt was over, and the dogs and game brought in, all the people crowded around the old fisherman, saying: 'What do you want of that hound? Better sell him; he's no good to you.'

They put the old man in a maze, there were so many of them, and they pressed him so hard.

He said at last: 'I'll sell the hound; and three hundred pounds is the price I want for him.'

'Here 'tis for you,' said a stranger, putting the money into his hand.

The old man took the money and gave up the dog, without taking off the rope. He forgot his son's warning.

That minute the Gruagach na g-cleasan called out: 'I'll take the worth of my money out of your son now;' and away he went with the hound.

The old man walked home alone that night, and it is a heavy heart he had in him when he came to the old woman without the son. And the two were lamenting their lot till morning.

Still and all, they were better off than the first time they lost their son, as they had plenty of everything, and could live at their ease.

The Gruagach went away home and put the fisherman's son in a cave of concealment that he had, bound him hand and foot, and tied hard knots on his neck up to the chin. From above there fell on him drops of poison, and every drop that fell went from the skin to the flesh, from the flesh to the bone, from the bone to the marrow, and he sat there under the poison drops, without meat, drink, or rest.

In the Gruagach's house was a servant-maid, and the fisherman's son had been kind to her the time he was in the place before.

On a day when the Gruagach and his eleven sons were out hunting, the maid was going with a tub of dirty water to throw it into the river that ran by the side of the house. She went through the cave of concealment where the fisherman's son was bound, and he asked of her the wetting of his mouth from the tub.

'Oh! The Gruagach would take the life of me,' said she, 'when he comes home, if I gave you as much as one drop.'

'Well,' said he, 'when I was in this house before, and when I had power in my hands, it's good and kind I was to you; and when I get out of this confinement I'll do you a turn, if you give me the wetting of my mouth now.'

The maid put the tub near his lips.

'Oh! I can't stoop to drink unless you untie one knot from my throat,' said he.

Then she put the tub down, stooped to him, and loosed one knot from his throat. When she loosened the one knot, he made an eel of himself, and dropped into the tub. There he began shaking the water, till he put some of it on the ground, and when he had the place about him wet,

109

he sprang from the tub, and slipped along out under the door.

The maid caught him; but could not hold him, he was so slippery. He made his way from the door to the river, which ran near the side of the house.

When the Gruagach na g-cleasan came home in the evening with his eleven sons, they went to take a look at the fisherman's son; but he was not to be seen.

Then the Gruagach called the maid, and taking his sword, said: 'I'll take the head off you if you don't tell me this minute what happened while I was gone.'

'Oh!' said the maid, 'he begged so hard for a drop of dirty water to wet his mouth that I hadn't the heart to refuse, for 'tis good he was to me and kind each time he saw me when he was here in the house before.

'When the water touched his mouth, he made an eel of himself, spilled water out of the tub, and slipped along over the wet place to the river outside. I caught him to bring him back, but I couldn't hold him; in spite of all I could do, he made away.'

The Gruagach dropped his sword and went to the water side with his sons.

The sons made eleven eels of themselves, and the Gruagach their father was the twelfth. They went around in the water, searching in every place, and there was not a stone in the river that they passed without looking under and around it for the old fisherman's son.

And when he knew that they were after him, he made himself into a salmon; and when they knew he was a salmon, the sons made eleven otters of themselves, and the Gruagach made himself the twelfth.

When the fisherman's son found that twelve otters were after him, he was weak with hunger, and when they had come near, he made himself a whale. But the eleven brothers and their father made twelve cannon whales of themselves, for they had all gone out of the river, and were in the sea now.

When they were coming near him, the fisherman's son was weak from pursuit and hunger, so he jumped up out of the water, and made a swallow of himself; but the Gruagach and his sons became twelve hawks and chased the swallow through the air; and as they whirled round and darted, they pressed him hard, till all of them came near the castle of the king of Erin.

Now the king had made a summerhouse for his daughter; and where should she be at this time but sitting on the top of the summerhouse.

The old fisherman's son dropped down till he was near her; then he fell into her lap in the form of a ring. The daughter of the king of Erin took up the ring, looked at it, and put it on her finger. The ring took her fancy, and she was glad.

When the Gruagach and his sons saw this, they let themselves down at the king's castle, having the form of the finest men that could be seen in the kingdom.

When the king's daughter had the ring on her finger, she looked at it and liked it. Then the ring spoke, and said: 'My life is in your hands now; don't part from the ring, and don't let it go to any man, and you'll give me a long life.'

The Gruagach na g-cleasan and his eleven sons went into the king's castle and played on every instrument known to man, and they showed every sport that could be shown before a king. This they did for three days and three nights. When that time was over, and they were going away, the king spoke up and asked: 'What is the reward that you would like, and what would be pleasing to you from me?'

'We want neither gold nor silver,' said the Gruagach; 'all the reward we ask of you is the ring that I lost on a time, and which is now on your daughter's finger.'

'If my daughter has the ring that you lost, it shall be given to you,' said the king.

Now the ring spoke to the king's daughter and said: 'Don't part with me for anything till you send your trusted man for three gallons of strong spirits and a gallon of wheat; put the spirits and the wheat together in an open barrel before the fire. When your father says you must give up the ring, do you answer back that you have never left the summerhouse, that you have nothing on your hand but what is your own and paid for. Your father will say then that you must part with me and give me up to the stranger. When he forces you in this way, and you can keep me no longer, then throw me into the fire; and you'll see great sport and strange things.'

The king's daughter sent for the spirits and the wheat, had them mixed together, and put in an open barrel before the fire.

The king called the daughter in, and asked: 'Have you the ring which this stranger lost?'

'I have a ring,' said she, 'but it's my own, and I'll not part with it. I'll not give it to him nor to any man.'

112

'You must,' said the king, 'for my word is pledged, and you must part with the ring!'

When she heard this, she slipped the ring from her finger and threw it into the fire.

That moment the eleven brothers made eleven pairs of tongs of themselves; their father, the old Gruagach, was the twelfth pair.

The twelve jumped into the fire to know in what spark of it would they find the old fisherman's son; and they were a long time working and searching through the fire, when out flew a spark, and into the barrel. The twelve made themselves men, turned over the barrel, and spilled the wheat on the floor. Then in a twinkling they were twelve cocks strutting around.

They fell to and picked away at the wheat to know which one would find the fisherman's son. Soon one dropped on one side, and a second on the opposite side, until all twelve were lying drunk from the wheat.

Then the old fisherman's son made a fox of himself, and the first cock he came to was the old Gruagach na g-cleasan himself. He took the head off the Gruagach with one bite, and the heads off the eleven brothers with eleven other bites.

When the twelve were dead, the old fisherman's son made himself the finest-looking man in Erin and began to give music and sport to the king; and he entertained him five times better than had the Gruagach and his eleven sons.

Then the king's daughter fell in love with him, and she set her mind on him to that degree that there was no life for her without him.

When the king saw the straits that his daughter was in, he ordered the marriage without delay.

The wedding lasted for nine days and nine nights, and the ninth night was the best of all.

When the wedding was over, the king felt he was losing his strength, so he took the crown off his own head, and put it on the head of the old fisherman's son and made him king of Erin in place of himself.

The young couple were the luck, and we the stepping-stones. The presents we got at the marriage were stockings of buttermilk and shoes of paper, and these were worn to the soles of our feet when we got home from the wedding.

From: Myths & Folk-Lore of Ireland

Blondine Lost

BLONDINE GREW TO be seven years old and Brunette three.

The king had given Blondine a charming little carriage drawn by ostriches, and a little coachman ten years of age, who was the nephew of her nurse.

The little page, who was called Gourmandinet, loved Blondine tenderly. He had been her playmate from her birth, and she had shown him a thousand acts of kindness.

But Gourmandinet had one terrible fault; he was a gourmand –was so fond of dainties and sweet things, that for a paper of bonbons he would commit almost any wicked action. Blondine often said to him: 'I love you dearly, Gourmandinet, but I do not love to see you so greedy. I entreat you to correct this villainous fault which will make you despised by all the world.'

Gourmandinet kissed her hand and promised to reform. But, alas! He continued to steal cakes from the kitchen and bonbons from the storeroom. Often, indeed, he was whipped for his disobedience and gluttony.

The queen Fourbette heard on every hand the reproaches lavished upon the page and she was cunning enough to think that she might make use of this weakness of Gourmandinet and thus get rid of poor Blondine.

The garden in which Blondine drove in her little carriage, drawn by ostriches and guided by her little coachman, Gourmandinet, was separated by a grating from an immense and magnificent forest, called the Forest of Lilacs because during the whole year these lilacs were always covered with superb flowers.

No one, however, entered these woods. It was well known that it was enchanted ground and that if you once entered there, you could never hope to escape.

Gourmandinet knew the terrible secret of this forest. He had been severely forbidden ever to drive the carriage of Blondine in that direction lest by some chance Blondine might pass the grating and place her little feet on the enchanted ground.

Many times, the king Benin had sought to build a wall the entire length of the grating or to secure it in some way so as to make an entrance there impossible. But the workmen had no sooner laid the foundation than some unknown and invisible power raised the stones and they disappeared from sight.

The queen Fourbette now sought diligently to gain the friendship of Gourmandinet by giving him every day some delicious dainties. In this way she made him so complete a slave to his appetite that he could not live without the jellies, bonbons and cakes which she gave him in such profusion.

At last, she sent for him to come to her, and said: 'Gourmandinet, it depends entirely upon yourself whether you shall have a large trunk full of bonbons and delicious dainties or never again eat one during your life.'

'Never again eat one! Oh! adam, I should die of such punishment. Speak, madam, what must I do to escape this terrible fate?'

'It is necessary,' said the queen, looking at him fixedly, 'that you should drive the princess Blondine near to the Forest of Lilacs.'

'I cannot do it, madam; the king has forbidden it.'

'Ah! You cannot do it; well, then, adieu. No more dainties for you. I shall command everyone in the house to give you nothing.'

'Oh! Madam,' said Gourmandinet, weeping bitterly, 'do not be so cruel. Give me some order which it is in my power to execute.'

'I can only repeat that I command you to lead the princess Blondine near to the Forest of Lilacs; that you encourage her to descend from the carriage, to cross the grating and enter the enchanted ground.'

'But, madam,' replied Gourmandinet, turning very pale, 'if the princess enters this forest, she can never escape from it. You know the penalty of entering upon enchanted ground. To send my dear princess there is to give her up to certain death.'

'For the third and last time,' said the queen, frowning fearfully, 'I ask if you will take the princess to the forest? Choose! Either an immense box of bonbons which I will renew every month or never again to taste the delicacies which you love.'

'But how shall I escape from the dreadful punishment which his majesty will inflict upon me?'

117

'Do not be disquieted on that account. As soon as you have induced Blondine to enter the Forest of Lilacs, return to me. I will send you off out of danger with your bonbons, and I charge myself with your future fortune.'

'Oh! Madam, have pity upon me. Do not compel me to lead my dear princess to destruction. She who has always been so good to me!'

'You still hesitate, miserable coward! Of what importance is the fate of Blondine to you? When you have obeyed my commands, I will see that you enter the service of Brunette and I declare to you solemnly that the bonbons shall never fail.'

Gourmandinet hesitated and reflected a few moments longer and alas! At last resolved to sacrifice his good little mistress to his gluttony.

The remainder of that day, he still hesitated and he lay awake all night weeping bitter tears as he endeavoured to discover some way to escape from the power of the wicked queen; but the certainty of the queen's bitter revenge if he refused to execute her cruel orders, and the hope of rescuing Blondine at some future day by seeking the aid of some powerful fairy, conquered his irresolution and decided him to obey the queen.

In the morning at ten o'clock, Blondine ordered her little carriage and entered it for a drive, after having embraced the king her father and promised him to return in two hours.

The garden was immense. Gourmandinet, on starting, turned the ostriches away from the Forest of Lilacs.

When, however, they were entirely out of sight of the palace, he changed his course and turned towards the grating which separated them from the enchanted ground. He was sad and silent. His crime weighed upon his heart and conscience.

'What is the matter?' said Blondine, kindly. 'You say nothing. Are you ill, Gourmandinet?'

'No, my princess, I am well.'

'But how pale you are! Tell me what distresses you, poor boy, and I promise to do all in my power to make you happy.'

Blondine's kind inquiries and attentions almost softened the hard heart of Gourmandinet, but the remembrance of the bonbons promised by the wicked queen, Fourbette, soon chased away his good resolutions. Before he had time to reply, the ostriches reached the grating of the Forest of Lilacs.

'Oh! The beautiful lilacs!' exclaimed Blondine; 'how fragrant – how delicious! I must have a bouquet of those beautiful flowers for my good papa. Get down, Gourmandinet and bring me some of those superb branches.'

'I cannot leave my seat, princess, the ostriches might run away with you during my absence.'

'Do not fear,' replied Blondine; 'I could guide them myself to the palace.'

'But the king would give me a terrible scolding for having abandoned you, princess. It is best that you go yourself and gather your flowers.'

'That is true. I should be very sorry to get you a scolding, my poor Gourmandinet.'

While saying these words she sprang lightly from the carriage, crossed the bars of the grating and commenced to gather the flowers.

At this moment, Gourmandinet shuddered and was overwhelmed with remorse. He wished to repair his fault by calling Blondine, but although she was only ten steps from him –although he saw her perfectly – she could not hear his voice, and in a short time she was lost to view in the enchanted forest.

For a long time Gourmandinet wept over his crime, cursed his gluttony and despised the wicked queen Fourbette.

At last, he recalled to himself that the hour approached at which Blondine would be expected at the palace. He returned to the stables through the back entrance and ran at once to the queen, who was anxiously expecting him.

On seeing him so deadly pale and his eyes inflamed from the tears of awful remorse, she knew that Blondine had perished.

'Is it done?' said she.

Gourmandinet bowed his head. He had not the strength to speak.

'Come,' said she, 'behold your reward!'

She pointed to a large box full of delicious bonbons of every variety. She commanded a valet to raise the box and place it upon one of the mules which had brought her jewellery.

'I confide this box to Gourmandinet, in order that he may take it to my father,' she said. 'Go, boy, and return in a month for another.'

She placed in his hand at the same time a purse full of gold.

Gourmandinet mounted the mule in perfect silence and set off in full gallop. The mule was obstinate and wilful and soon grew restive under the weight of the box and began to prance and kick. He did this so effectually that he threw Gourmandinet and his precious box of bonbons upon the ground.

Gourmandinet, who had never ridden upon a horse or mule, fell heavily with his head upon the stones and died instantly.

Thus, he did not receive from his crime the profit which he had hoped, for he had not even tasted of the bonbons which the queen had given him.

No one regretted him.

No one but the poor Blondine had ever loved him.

From: Old French Fairy Tales

Finis

Workbooks From The Scheherazade Foundation

We hope that you have enjoyed this collection of stories, gleaned from varying cultural corners of the world, and that you have been entertained by them.

But, have you considered the deeper meanings and interwoven layers that lie hidden beneath the surface?

At The Scheherazade Foundation, we believe that Teaching-Stories contain wisdom, information, and marvels that have the power to transform the way we think, and thereby change our lives.

Employed as a bedrock of culture throughout the centuries – challenging established patterns of thinking, while passing on knowledge and values – tales such as the ones contained in this volume are a rich resource ready and waiting to be mined.

As an aid to help in the perception of less-obvious facets and layers, we have created a series of original Workbooks. Aimed at stimulating thought-provoking discussions and igniting deep reflection, these tools will assist in unlocking the power of Teaching-Stories.